P9-DMR-412

Praise for Amanda Cross
and *The Edge of Doom*

"No one has a sharper eye than Amanda Cross."
—*The Washington Post Book World*

"For those who deplore the decline of the classic whodunit . . . the news is good. Amanda Cross is back. . . . Cross is a graceful and sophisticated writer, whose relatively bloodless novels depend for their excitement on the clash of personalities rather than the exchange of bullets. Those who fondly remember the Good Old Days will relish this opportunity to revisit them."
—*The San Diego Union-Tribune*

"Like a good mystery? Try Amanda Cross's *The Edge of Doom*. A twisty, turny plot that would make a box office bonanza."
—King Features Syndicate

"This thought piece from [Amanda Cross] burnishes and deepens the character of New Yorker, feminist, and literature professor Kate Fansler. . . . Very satisfying on both an intellectual and an emotional level."
—*Booklist*

"Excellent reading . . . This elegantly written mystery is delightfully witty and full of intriguing Shakespearean allusions to fathers and daughters."
—*Deadly Pleasures*

By Amanda Cross
Published by Ballantine Books:

THE THEBAN MYSTERIES
POETIC JUSTICE
DEATH IN A TENURED POSITION
IN THE LAST ANALYSIS
THE JAMES JOYCE MURDER
THE QUESTION OF MAX
SWEET DEATH, KIND DEATH
NO WORD FROM WINIFRED
A TRAP FOR FOOLS
THE PLAYERS COME AGAIN
AN IMPERFECT SPY
THE COLLECTED STORIES
THE PUZZLED HEART
HONEST DOUBT
THE EDGE OF DOOM

Books published by The Random House Publishing Group
are available at quantity discounts on bulk purchases for
premium, educational, fund-raising, and special sales use.
For details, please call 1-800-733-3000.

THE EDGE OF
DOOM

AMANDA
CROSS

FAWCETT BOOKS • NEW YORK

Sale of this book without a front cover may be unauthorized. If this book is coverless, it may have been reported to the publisher as "unsold or destroyed" and neither the author nor the publisher may have received payment for it.

A Fawcett Book
Published by The Random House Publishing Group

Copyright © 2002 by Carolyn G. Heilbrun

All rights reserved under International and Pan-American Copyright Conventions. Published in the United States by The Random House Publishing Group, a division of Random House, Inc., New York, and simultaneously in Canada by Random House of Canada Limited, Toronto.

The Edge of Doom is a work of fiction. Names, places, and incidents either are a product of the author's imagination or are used fictitiously.

Fawcett and colophon are registered trademarks of Random House, Inc.

www.ballantinebooks.com

ISBN 0-345-45237-2

Manufactured in the United States of America

First Hardcover Edition: November 2002
First Mass Market Edition: November 2003

OPM   10   9   8   7   6   5   4   3   2   1

To Tom Driver
Sir, my good friend; I'll change that name with you.

THE EDGE OF
DOOM

One

KATE FANSLER would have said, had anybody asked, that she rarely heard from her brothers these days, or they from her. Eleven, eight, and six years older than she, the senior among them was now past his sixty-seventh birthday. She and her brothers had rarely agreed about anything, though the passing years had brought some air of tolerance to their infrequent meetings, or perhaps it was only the final acceptance of the fact that they would never agree and had better discuss neutral subjects. Alas, there were few of these.

Even the weather, once innocent of causing political dissent, now stimulated mention of the greenhouse effect, the hole in the ozone layer, and the dangers threatened by the use of fossil fuels. Nor were Kate's nieces and nephews, as a subject of conversation, beyond contention. On the whole, their views were closer to Kate's than to their fathers'; even on that topic composure was likely to fail. In

1

fact, Kate rarely thought of her brothers and confidently assumed that they returned the favor.

Her surprise, therefore, on receiving a letter from Laurence, her oldest brother, was profound. For this was not an invitation to a party, or even to a lunch during which money might possibly be discussed, but a request for Kate to meet him at his club on a "personal" matter. Kate grinned at that. Laurence had been one of the most adamant against the admission of women to all-male clubs, and here he was inviting his sister to meet him in those very precincts without, if she knew Laurence, even reflecting on the exaggerated fears of women in his club that had formerly haunted him.

The request was for Friday afternoon; Kate could guess why. The club would be less populated, and Laurence would be able usefully to pass the time before contemplating the weekend's activities. He had been forced by his law firm's long-standing and unalterable rules to retire at sixty-five, but because of his prominence in the firm and his still impressive connections, he was permitted to occupy an office—not, of course, the elegant corner one he had claimed in his prime, but an office nonetheless—to go to, to go home from, there to enjoy the occasional services of a secretary. Laurence, Kate could well surmise, had hated having to retire.

Kate was surprised to find herself puzzling over this invitation. She had some time ago come to the dreary conclusion that life could no longer offer the unexpected—except, of course, for those debilitating and often sudden bodily assaults common to aging; these could hardly be called unexpected, however impossible exactly to anticipate. And here, lo and

2

behold, was an invitation from Laurence to meet at his club.

Kate could imagine no rational explanation for this astonishing summons. Laurence might be lonely—she suspected he had always been lonely, though perhaps not aware of it—but she would be the last person sent for to allay that suffering. He could hardly have decided to call money "personal," nor could she imagine any reason why he might wish to discuss that subject, long since clarified between them. Kate had convinced him that she did not need his financial advice or counsel, nor did she welcome it. What else was there? Family problems? His wife Janice? But in no case Kate could think of was Kate the one—indeed she was probably the last one—to be called upon to deal with questions of his immediate family.

Well, it was a small surprise, she thought, calling to leave a message for Laurence to say she would meet him at the time and place mentioned, but it hardly qualified as an event. No, she was past interesting surprises in any area of life—of that she was certain. Not the academic world, nor global crises, nor territorial or religious wars, nor any call upon her abilities in literature or detection was likely to provide her with an expectation of what might be involved. There were no more surprises. Even Laurence, she supposed, would not really be a surprise; he would have thought of some hideously uninteresting, magnificently unstartling reason to speak with her.

Which goes to suggest that certainty on any matter is not one of the human attitudes the gods admire

3

or tolerate. Kate should have remembered her Greek myths.

Laurence greeted her with all the awkwardness of near relatives who neither like each other nor often meet. He offered her a drink and ordered one for himself. Well, Kate thought, we both drink Scotch; I suppose that's something. Laurence had commandeered a corner spot promising privacy, although the club's conversations, if at all extended, were private; it was that kind of club.

In its ambience and furnishings, the room they were in was redolent of masculinity. There was no elephant head mounted on the wall, as at the Harvard Club, nor were there portraits of male administrators as at the Yale Club. The leather chairs were large, as befitted ample male bottoms, and the service staff was both male and obsequious. Kate, who was tall, nonetheless sank back in her chair, forced either to recline rather further than she would have chosen, or to sit firmly upright. Most of the men seemed to lean forward as they partook of conversations with other men.

They sat in silence until the drinks arrived, Kate observing her surroundings and Laurence looking as though he wanted to say something unimportant and pleasant, but found himself unable to decide on the appropriate subject. Kate wondered what he would have chatted about with a male colleague from Wall Street. When the drinks arrived, served with a flourish, and accompanied by a dish of nuts, she and Laurence raised their glasses in a mild salute. Kate settled down to listen.

"What do you think of Edith Wharton?" Laurence asked.

"What?" Kate said.

"Edith Wharton, the writer. Surely you've heard of her. You are a professor of literature, aren't you?"

"Indubitably," Kate said. "The question is: why should you care what I think of Edith Wharton?"

"Because I think you have a lot in common with her."

Laurence could hardly have asked a question likely to astonish her more. If the club doorman had come up to inquire about her views on Jane Austen, Kate would have been less surprised than to hear her brother Laurence, who thought literature fancy stuff and very unmanly, bringing up Edith Wharton. As to that famous writer and Kate having anything in common, well, beyond respect for the English language—Kate took a rather larger sip from her drink, a sip almost qualifying as a gulp, and decided to meet Laurence on the ground he had chosen.

"Edith Wharton," she began, setting down her glass, "was born in 1860 or thereabouts into one of those dreadful wealthy and well-established families at a time when girls didn't attend school and didn't do anything later in life except marry; her marriage was miserable. She wrote excellent novels, but she was forty before she published her first one. She lived abroad most of her life and built that amazing summer home in the Berkshires. What else? Laurence, she and I have absolutely nothing in common. Why on earth are we discussing her?"

Laurence sipped his drink and smiled in a rather

5

satisfied way, as when one knows one has something interesting to impart and anticipates imparting it. "She had love affairs, she had no children, she had a private income, and she admired Henry James. It seems to me that's rather a lot you two shared." And he looked remarkably pleased with himself.

Kate stared at him. "Laurence," she said, "please stop smirking and tell me why we are here having this conversation. I'm willing to wager that you've never so much as mentioned Edith Wharton before. When did you get up all these facts about her? And speaking of what Edith Wharton and I have in common, did you happen to notice that she died about ten years before I was born?"

"I didn't say you knew her," Laurence said. "I just mentioned that you had a lot in common."

Kate began to suspect a brain tumor, so utterly uncharacteristic was Laurence's interest in a woman writer, to say nothing of his extensive knowledge of her life. Did brain tumors usually take this literary form?

"Never mind," Laurence said, looking more serious. "I'm just joshing you. I really have to tell you something."

"To do with Edith Wharton?"

"In a way." Laurence summoned the waiter for a second round of drinks, having offered Kate another which she had eagerly accepted; he now seemed to be wondering how to start the conversation over. Kate half expected, half feared to have references to Willa Cather thrust upon her.

"Edith Wharton had older brothers," he said, after a pause.

"Laurence," Kate began. "I admit it: Edith Wharton and I both had older brothers. She only had two, as I remember; I, you will recall, have three."

Kate was rather ashamed to find herself so ungracious with Laurence, and determined to change her tone of voice to one more pleasant or, at least, less impatient.

Laurence seemed unmoved by her uneasy tone, or perhaps he had not noticed it. "Her mother was rather stiff and proper," he said.

Kate tried to keep her tone even. "Yes, Laurence, our mother was proper but not stiff. Conventional, yes, but much more emotional than Wharton's. Laurence, please"—she could not refrain from adding—"for the sake of my sanity, get to the point."

"The point is"—he seemed to have to force himself to say it—"that Edith Wharton's birth so long after her brothers' gave rise to some speculation."

"So it did. It's been surmised that it might have been the brothers' tutor who was the seducer. But it's all nonsense; people love mysteries."

"Why wasn't there a child in between?" Laurence asked.

"There may have been miscarriages." Kate was now past even the pretense of congeniality. "Laurence, what are you trying to say?"

And then Kate got it. "You can't be serious," she said. "Are you suggesting that our mother, that I, that—Laurence, are you going in for romance in your later years? You can't be suggesting what I think you're suggesting."

But then Kate remembered that in fact this particular comparison with Edith Wharton had been made before in the family, a kind of joke about how different Kate was from all the rest of the Fanslers. She couldn't now remember who had first mentioned Edith Wharton in connection with Kate, but no doubt that was what had brought Wharton to Laurence's attention. Asking his wife or secretary to pick up a book on her had been no trouble; the Louis Auchincloss book must have been an obvious choice.

"Laurence, why are you bringing all this up at this moment?" Laurence sank back into his large leather chair with a smile of evident satisfaction. "I'm not suggesting your resemblance to Edith Wharton in this matter," he said pontifically. "I know it for a fact."

"You know! And you've waited all these years to tell me about this suspicion? What did you do, walk in on them while—Laurence, I can't believe this of you. It can't be your idea of a joke."

"Of course I didn't walk in on them. I never thought of any such thing. This man came to my office the other day and announced that he was your father. That he had been our mother's lover. That's how I know. Of course, I threw him out."

"Literally?" Kate asked, entranced at the thought.

"No. He said he was leaving and could save me the trouble of throwing him out. Then he said that he was not after anything, he just wanted me, as the oldest son, to tell you because he was leaving you quite a lot of money. He said he had seen you upon occasion—giving a lecture, he said—and he had read your writings. He thought you were a worthy daughter. His words."

"He's obviously crackers," Kate said, enjoying a

rush of relief. Poor Laurence had taken all this seriously.

"He said he would have DNA tests done. He said if you would prick your finger and give him some blood, he would prove it. He would send me the laboratory report; I can check up on it. He said it will prove he's related to you, that he's definitely your father."

Kate snorted, an unladylike expression she had acquired since her proper girlhood. "And you believed all this nonsense, and even went so far as to read a life of Edith Wharton. What made you think of Edith Wharton?"

"He suggested I read about her. I found something on her by Louis Auchincloss."

"A literary critic born into the upper class; how appropriate." Kate realized she was on the verge of becoming rude, had, in fact, become rude, perhaps to avoid serious worry about Laurence. Had he imagined the whole thing? "I remember Louis Auchincloss on Wharton," she said. "He didn't believe the tutor thing for a minute. Who, after all, could imagine a young man approaching Edith Wharton's mother with sexual intentions? The whole idea is absurd."

"But you said our mother was nicer than Edith Wharton's mother," Laurence said, but almost as though he had lost interest. Clearly, he was past arguing; he shrugged. "Look, Kate," he said, "I haven't mentioned this to anyone. It seemed wiser to tell you first. If you want to go to the ladies' room and prick your finger and get a little blood on a Kleenex, I'll give it to him and that will settle the whole matter. Why not?"

9

Kate was at first amused to think that she had to retire to the ladies' room to bleed on a piece of Kleenex; one could hardly, it appeared, prick oneself in the club lounge. Then she began to ponder it. Well, what could be the harm? This wasn't like those novels of long ago where people with no evidence claimed to be the lost child or father of other people, as in Dickens' novels and in Shakespeare's plays. We had DNA now. So what the hell.

"All right, I'll go to the ladies' room—but I don't have anything to prick myself with," she said.

"I've brought a needle," Laurence answered, producing it. He had planned this whole thing carefully. If he was ill, it was a serious matter.

Well, Kate thought, at the worst I will make a fool of myself. Reed and I can laugh about it. She took the needle Laurence held out, and went off to provide a blood sample. "But," she said to Laurence, "I shall expect to find another drink waiting for me when I return. Losing blood is a serious business."

But not as serious as losing your mind, she thought, walking from the room.

*Thou art thy father's daughter;
there's enough.*

Two

"**W**HAT ON EARTH shall I do?" Kate asked Reed, as they sat in their living room, having their evening drink, Kate with her feet up, Banny, their Saint Bernard, feet tucked under, lying on the floor beside her. Reed, who preferred a more upright position, sat on the couch across from the other two.

"Get expert advice, I should think," he said.

"Is there something sinister he can do with that sample of my blood?" Kate asked. "Should I not have given it to him?"

"Apart from comparing your DNA with that of whomever he may choose, there's not much he can do with it—unless, that is, you believe in the older forms of witchcraft."

"What on earth do you mean?"

"A poor joke, Kate. Aren't you letting this upset you unduly? I admit your brother's news was startling, but until you know who this man is, why not ignore the whole thing?"

11

"Ignore the fact that either some man is approaching me for nefarious purposes or, which is probably worse, that my mother, that I . . . ?" She was unable to finish the sentence.

"Well, look at it this way. You and everybody else have always noticed that you're nothing like your brothers. 'Nothing like' is a serious understatement; you couldn't possibly be more different in every possible way."

"I have been said to bear some physical resemblance to one or the other of them in the past," Kate pointed out.

"No one's saying you didn't all have the same mother." Reed got up to refill their glasses. "Kate, I know this is a bit of a shock, and you are wondering why you toddled off to the ladies' room to prick your finger as though mesmerized. Let's wait to see what this man says are the results."

"We can't take his word for it."

"Of course not. We'll find ourselves a DNA expert and have it all rechecked."

"And if he does turn out to be my father?"

"I think that's not only rather exciting, it also explains a good deal. I'm actually eager to meet this man, if he is your father, or even if he wants to be. And remember, he wants to leave you money, not con you out of yours."

"That," Kate said, "may just be the beginning of a con game."

"Naturally that occurred to me," Reed said. "But you, to say nothing of myself, are not a likely victim of a con artist."

"Suppose," Kate said, "he turns out to be my fa-

12

ther, and then needs me to support him. Have you thought of that?"

"Kate. Dear, sweet Kate. You've given the man, or anyway your brother, a drop of your blood. I promise you it will lead to nothing terrifying, other than"—he held up an admonishing finger as Kate yelped an interruption—"what ideas may be stirred up by proof that he is in fact your father."

"I've been doing arithmetic," Kate said. "Counting on my fingers, mostly. My mother was born in 1914—nearly a century ago. Imagine! She was thirty-six when I was born. Wasn't that considered rather late to have a child in those days? I don't seem to have thought about it before. She was only twenty-one when Laurence was born."

"Thirty-six may have been late then for a first child," Reed said. "Perhaps not for a fourth."

"I didn't know you were an expert on human fertility."

"I think you're letting this affect you inordinately, Kate. You usually don't get carried away and testy."

"You're right; I'm sorry. I can't imagine why this is causing so forceful a reaction. It's as though I've been told I may be someone other than I thought I was. Do you suppose this is what it's like to discover you're adopted?"

"Probably. I think that's why adoptive parents today let the child know it's adopted very early on."

"Really, Reed, no testiness is intended. But you do seem to be a fountain of familial information."

"Odd bits of information turn up in the D.A.'s office where I spent so many long days, and some of

them even take on significance. DNA is hardly unknown in connection with the criminal world. Anyway, everything I've mentioned is commonplace in
newspapers these days. You know it all too, if you
think about it."

"I'm not sure I want to think about it. Let's talk
about something else; something very clearly else."

And they did, for that evening at least. But as
they talked, Kate found herself overwhelmed in a
way she would not have thought possible. Why, after all, was this news so stupendous?

By the next day Reed had unearthed a friend who
was a DNA expert, or enough of one to satisfy
Reed's purposes and Kate's. He had promised to report to Reed on e-mail, and did so. Reed had asked
him a specific question: assuming a man (Reed had
put his inquiry in general terms) claimed to be the
father of a certain woman, could DNA testing, for
example, distinguish between the man as the father
of the woman and the man as the half brother of the
woman? For it had occurred to Reed that this man
might actually be a by-blow of Kate's father; in that
case his DNA would certainly establish a connection with her. He had mentioned this possibility to
Kate, who had silently rolled her eyes and only demanded to know the results when Reed had got
them in hand.

The results had arrived at his office in the afternoon, and he handed the printout to Kate as soon
as he was inside the door. She had been loitering
about near the front door, expecting him, unable to
settle to anything or even to stay seated in one

place. Banny, regarding her with an obviously troubled expression, turned her head from side to side as though watching a tennis match.

When Reed arrived to find her at the door, he looked as troubled as the dog. "For God's sake, Kate," he said, taking off his coat and reaching into his briefcase, "don't you think you're overreacting just a bit?"

"Of course I'm overreacting, and what's more, I don't know why I'm overreacting. What possible difference can it make, over half a century later, if I turn out to be the result of one sperm instead of another, or if my mother, whom I thought of as the height of conventionality, and who was, after all, born not that far from the last century, was screwing around?"

"All right," Reed said, "what difference is it making, or threatening to make?"

"I haven't a clue, so don't ask. My questions are rhetorical. Where's the damn report?"

Reed handed it to her. "Let's sit down," he said. "The answer to my question is clear enough, though the explanation is hard-going, becoming quite complicated and esoteric."

Kate took the sheet of paper from Reed, and sat down to read it. She did not put her feet up. He saw her read through it and then begin again. The doctor had clearly considered Reed's request about the man's being a possible half brother to Kate as the substantive question. If the man were indeed the father of the woman in question, he had told Reed, there would be no doubt about it. He had further written:

"It is possible to discern a father-daughter relationship from a half brother–half sister relationship. First, consider the X chromosomes."

Kate made what she hoped was an intelligent effort to consider the X chromosomes, before deciding that this was a waste of time. She read on; the doctor had decided to use himself as an example:

"My daughter has two X chromosomes. One of them comes from me, and one comes from my wife. If my daughter were in fact my half sister and we shared the same father, as in the case you are asking about, it would not be possible for her to have the same X chromosome as me, because I inherited my X from my mother, who is unrelated to her."

Kate looked up. "Yes," she said, "I think I've got that. More or less. This reminds me of Charles Sanger's demonstration that Emily Brontë really knew inheritance law when she had Heathcliff inherit everything from both families."

"I'm glad to see you're sounding more like yourself," Reed said. "When you mention literature, I know sanity is not far away."

Kate read on: "The answer for the twenty-two other chromosomes, called autosomes, is more complicated but also definitive. Sorry about the technospeak, but it's the only way to be accurate. Here goes: For a given pair of alleles carried by my daughter, it is certain that one of them comes from me. If she were my half sister, there would be a 50 percent chance that the allele she inherited from our shared father is not the same allele that I inherited from him. If we consider allelic pairs from each of the twenty-two autosomes, there is only about a one in 4.2 million chance that my half sister and I would inherit the same twenty-two alleles from our father. So if you assess RFLPs at twenty-two loci, one on each autosome, and find that in all twenty-two cases the woman and man share an allele, then she is his daughter to a certainty of one in four million. Another way of looking at this is that in the father-daughter pair, the daughter has half of the father's DNA, while in the half-sibling case, the two each have half of their father's DNA, but not the same half."

"What is an RFLP?" Kate asked.

"I don't know," Reed said, "but it seems that the conclusion is clear enough. If this man is your father, that will be readily apparent. If he is your half brother—and after all that's just a possibility that came to my mind with no basis in fact—then we'll know that, too. So at least evidence from the DNA will be clear enough."

"Well, whatever that man says the report says, I think we had better have it done over. We'll have to ask him to prick his finger into some Kleenex. After all, fair's fair."

"I'm sure he will see it that way," Reed said. "Now how about concentrating on the fact that whether he's your father or not will not alter a single moment of your life up to now. You are still the Kate Fansler who has lived so far. What it may change in your perception of your parents is another matter, I do realize. But that, dear Kate, is in the past. The long ago, over half a century past."

"Is it all right if I wonder about what my mother was up to?"

17

"Wonder away. But until we know the results of all this DNA business, we can't be sure she was up to anything."

"You realize he must have been much younger than she. Probably he was the age of her oldest son, or very near to it."

"Well, good for your mother, but I doubt he was Laurence's age, which was eleven when you were born. She undoubtedly was a most attractive woman even past the height of youth, as you are."

"Nicely put, Reed. I can hardly wait to meet the man."

"Do you want to meet him only if he is your father, or do you think he will be interesting in himself?"

"I guess I want to know why he would play this charade if he isn't my father; and I need to know all about him if he is."

"We do have to remember that Laurence may be undergoing a senior moment, as I believe they are now called. There may be no such man at all." Reed went to prepare their drinks.

"The trouble is," Kate said, "I don't know what to hope for. As T. S. Eliot put it, 'wait without hope, for hope would be hope for the wrong thing.' But it's a little hard to know what the wrong thing might be in this case."

"Or the right thing, either," Reed muttered, as they settled down in the living room. "I didn't know you liked T. S. Eliot."

Kate smiled her appreciation at his trying to change the subject, enticing her to talk about poetry, which she loved but rarely taught and never wrote about.

"T. S. Eliot the man seems a frightful creature; he

probably always was," Kate said. "But the poet, alas, that is something else."

"I used to feel that way about baseball players," Reed said. "I know it sounds frivolous, but it was a great shock to me as a boy and even after that to discover what awful men some of my favorite players were. It took me a while to understand that one can love and admire the game, or the poetry, and not care for, in fact ignore, the players and the poets. It's nice to discover that a great shortstop is a sweet guy, but it's his elegant moves as a shortstop that one relishes."

"That's right," Kate said, but Reed could tell her mind was wandering back to her possible paternity. "Shall we eat in tonight?" Kate asked, getting to her feet. Reed nodded, and they both went into the kitchen, bringing their glasses. "I guess even Joe Di-Maggio has turned out to be a quite unlovable guy with a good sense of marketing himself," Kate said, still trying to stick to any other subject, baseball as it had turned out.

"Well, he was a Yankee," Reed said, keeping up his end, "so what could you expect? I was a Giants fan."

"Are you still?" Kate evidently was determined to spin out this discussion so kindly started by Reed; it could hardly last very long, of course, as Reed understood.

"The Giants moved to the West Coast," he said. He had never taken very seriously the possibility of interesting Kate in baseball, or any other spectator sport. But he was amused by her determination to "make conversation," an undertaking they had never before felt the need of. "I've always been a National

League person," he said. "The very idea of the designated hitter offends me."

Kate looked puzzled.

"Don't ask," Reed said. "It's not really easy to explain. Are you feeling any better?"

"A little saner, I think. There is some chicken left; is that okay?"

"Fine."

"What I can't get out of my head," Kate said, removing dishes from the refrigerator, "is that the person I am is in part due to someone I've never met or known about."

"The person you are is due to you," Reed said. "You are what you made yourself. I grant you all the facts about genetics, but plenty of women your age with the same genes might have turned out very differently."

"We can't know that."

"Granted. We can't know anything, so why brood about it? And don't reheat the chicken; let's eat it cold."

"What I keep thinking of, Reed, is the woman I might have been if what this man claims is true. Suppose I had been the child of my putative father, if you see what I mean. I might have lived in the suburbs, and had three children, and taken courses in flower arranging."

"I can't imagine that, no matter who your father was."

"It's still a pretty shocking prospect," Kate said.

"But not frightening surely. I should think you'd feel glad to have escaped such a fate. Not that it's a bad fate, but it hardly suits you."

"It's what might have suited me that I keep thinking about," Kate said. "What I might have been. All the other hopes and desires I might have had."

"What you need," Reed said, "is another drink."

That thou art my [daughter], I have partly thy mother's word, partly my own opinion; but chiefly a villanous trick of thine eye and a foolish hanging of thy nether lip, that doth warrant me.

Three

IN THE DAYS following, Kate's thoughts as she went about her work intermittently returned, as of their own volition, to conjectures about genes. This was not a subject on which she was highly informed, nor did she seem to wish to undertake extensive research, or indeed any research, on the matter. Research, in Kate's view, had to have a purpose, and she could not at the moment see any purpose in the gathering of genetic information. Keeping her mind on her job was effort enough and, on the whole, successful. But in between, the same themes emerged.

She knew the work of so-called sociobiologists who saw genes as the dominant, probably the only force behind individual actions, and the work of those more liberal who, by emphasis on upbringing and environment, countered such theories, finding them racist and socially biased. Between these alternatives she wandered, first convinced of genetic dominance, then persuaded by the force of cultural and social pressures. In short, when not teaching literature or coping with the responsibilities of academia, Kate convinced herself one moment that who her father was hardly signified, made little difference to who she had become, and at another moment felt certain that what had formerly seemed, in her opposition to her family's doctrines, as originality on her part was little more than different genes at work. She did not yet know if her genes were different, less Fansler than she had supposed, or if she was simply who she had always supposed herself to be. And so she speculated, her thoughts chasing one another circuitously and pointlessly.

Teaching literature in her seminars, she managed to keep her mind on the texts and the students, but questions would intrude: how explain George Eliot, no more like her family than Kate was like the Fanslers? The Brontës, on the other hand, had each other, the moors, their isolation; they seemed to share the same mysterious source of talent. But was not such talent always hard to account for? Not so, Kate reminded herself before her office hours, with musicians or mathematicians, whose amazing talents, manifesting themselves at an early age, seemed almost always to be inherited.

She, Kate, had after all proceeded through her twenties hand in hand, as it were, with the march of feminism, an influence unlikely to have affected her brothers or her parents, and probably sufficient to account for her deviations from them.

Walking home in the hope that exercise and air would clear her head, she considered twins. Who had not heard stories of identical twins raised apart who turned out, meeting as adults, to be wearing identical ties and to each have a dog named Eddie? Well, no one doubted that genes existed, but the human chromosome endowment was so large, who could say whence came what trait? And what about adopted children, who got on with life as life should be got on with, as a living present and not an endowment from the past?

Kate opened the front door of their apartment to find herself greeted by Banny and Reed, both lingering uncharacteristically in the hall.

"Is something wrong?" Kate asked, forgetting about genes and thinking only of disaster.

"Not at all," Reed said. "We just wanted to be sure we would hear you come in."

"About the DNA?" Kate now asked, recovering herself.

"Yes," Reed said. "I just got off the phone with Laurence. He asked for you but seemed willing to talk with me. Relieved, in fact, to tell the truth."

"And?" Kate urged, as Reed paused.

"That man does seem to be your father. He is also not your half brother, an idea of mine reflecting my ignorance of the finer points of DNA, without basis or, it transpires, without substance. Of course, as Laurence suggested and I agreed, new samples from both of you must be tested. But one does rather have the impression that you are a Fansler in name only."

"Well, that's over then. Now we know." Kate, rather to her surprise, found herself content with the result. What dramatists we all are, and you especially, she said to herself, mocking. What a letdown it would have been to be just what you always were, with nothing new and challenging to disrupt your life.

Something of this must have shown in her face, because Reed grinned and took her hand, leading her into the living room. Kate, still holding on to her bag, dropped it in the hall. "Adventures are always fun," Reed said, "as is speculation in the right conditions. Apart from your brothers, whose reaction to this news, if true, I can hardly envision, there is nothing much to worry about, and you can stop saying that life holds no more surprises. I call this surprise a dilly."

"Are we to know his name?" Kate asked when Reed had poured their drinks and she had at last sat down, allowing Banny to collapse at her feet with a grateful sigh.

"That's about all we know," Reed said. "Laurence almost forgot to ask him his name, doubtless, as I suspect, bowled over by the DNA report. I think your brother didn't really believe the man's story for a moment, and is quite rocked by this proof—which Laurence doesn't doubt, by the way— proof about you and his sainted mother. I hope you'll forgive me for referring to her in so discourteous a way."

"His name?" Kate demanded, ignoring this.

"Ah. Well, that's rather a shock, too. His name is Jason Ebenezer Smith. Everyone calls him Jay."

"Ebenezer! Laurence is incapable of making that up. Are you being cute, Reed? I must say that isn't like you."

"I am never cute," Reed said with mock dignity. "The man, Jay, gave his name as Jason E. Smith—

that was the name on the letter that came with the DNA report—and Laurence demanded to know what the *E* was for. No doubt he was hoping against hope that something would prove the whole business untrue. So Jay E. Smith told him his middle name was Ebenezer."

"And of course Laurence didn't know enough to ask a question about Dickens. He or you might have quoted Shakespeare: 'I cannot tell what the dickens his name is.' And I still can't get over his reading up on Edith Wharton."

"No, apparently he didn't catch the Dickens connection. And I don't believe that's a Shakespeare quote."

"You can look it up. But why would anyone name a child after Scrooge?"

"Well, he did reform in the end, after all, and buy that huge turkey. Or was it a goose? Jay's parents might have thought they needed something rather unusual to go with Smith. Or, here's a thought: Maybe he was born on Christmas. You can ask him when you meet, after we get confirmation of these results."

"You don't doubt them, do you?"

"No. It would make no sense as some sort of con game. Your brother may not be very up on his literary references, but just given who he is and the firm he's a part of, someone would have to be balmy to try to put this sort of thing over on him as a swindle."

"I expect you're right. Well," Kate finally put her feet up and seemed to relax slightly, "while we're waiting for the confirmation, I'll try to think what to ask him when we meet. There are many obvious questions, even exciting ones, but I think I'll begin with why he's called Ebenezer."

"It does prove," Reed said, "that unlike Laurence, his parents had read Dickens. He may not have been your brothers' tutor, since they didn't have one, but he probably wasn't the gamekeeper either. All this is ridiculous speculation; I shall be silent and await news of your encounter with your father."

"I still can't quite believe it," Kate said.

"You might consider the definition of a father. Is he the man who oversees his child's life from birth to maturity, or the man who happens to have been in the room when his child was conceived?"

"I'm sure there's some kind of definition between those two," Kate said, "even leaving biology and genes out of the picture."

"Perhaps. Your second question might be whether he ever met you before your meeting now."

"I shall ask that, of course. But all this has started me thinking about my Fansler father. He wasn't the most attentive parent on earth, but given the period in which he lived, when fathers like him were expected to spend their weekdays at the office and their weekends on the golf course, he wasn't inattentive. He did seem pleased that I was a girl. Now that I think of it, they had rather hoped my youngest brother would be a girl. How did I know that? One of the things children pick up, no doubt. I expect it's what made David so macho, much more so than William, the middle brother."

"David's a Dickensian name," Reed pointed out.

"Perhaps Jay was around for that birth and suggested it. You don't suppose . . ."

27

"Not for a minute. Remember, I've met David a number of times, and if he looked much more like the pictures of your father I've seen, he would be a clone. And Dickens hardly had a copyright on the name David."

"Unlike Ebenezer. Well, that's a relief anyway."

"Good," Reed said. "Of course your parents may have seen the movie of *David Copperfield*, the long-ago one, with W. C. Fields and Freddie Bartholomew. 'Another boy: What shall we call him? What about that nice movie we saw the other night?' "

"I'm not sure my parents ever went to the movies; I suppose they must have, really. I used to go with my governess to approved films."

"Your brother David is named after a movie; that's my story and I stick to it."

And to Reed's relief, they both laughed and went on to speak of the day's happenings in their usual manner.

The question was where were Kate and her father Jay to meet? When speaking with Reed she had tried calling her father Ebenezer but soon found Jay came more readily to the tongue; also *Ebenezer* when often said seemed to occupy an inordinate amount of time. That Jay Ebenezer Smith was her father had been twice confirmed, and meet they must. After dismissing several venues, Kate had decided on the Oak Room at the Plaza; challenged she could not defend this choice, but felt it the appropriate ambience for so Victorian an event as meeting, in middle age, one's father for the first time. This, however, was not to be.

Laurence had taken on the role of sponsor to this

odd encounter; he called it a reunion, but Kate was not yet certain if she and Jay Ebenezer had ever had a first meeting, however long ago. Whether because he clung to lurid doubts of Jay's intentions which no DNA test could erase, or whether he was simply curious and unwilling to miss out on a dramatic moment was hard to determine. Nonetheless, Laurence claimed the role of host to this meeting, and insisted it must take place at his club where he had first broken the news of Jay's paternity to Kate. Kate suspected that Laurence had not yet told the rest of the Fanslers, including his wife and brothers, about Jay and wished to have an ample report when he came to do so, including the first meeting of father and daughter.

Reed, agreeing with her interpretation, urged her to acquiesce. Meeting one's father for what was probably the first time at so late a date might best be undertaken, he argued, in the presence of a third person. Why deprive Laurence of the pleasure of introducing the two of them to one another? There were, as Kate had to admit, few enough significant human events in Laurence's life—events, Reed meant, not dehumanized by elaborate ceremonies and celebrations—so that one hesitated to deprive him of this one.

So Kate went yet again to meet Laurence at his club. She had agreed to arrive some minutes before Jay Ebenezer, and indeed found Laurence in the same corner they had occupied previously, as though, Kate thought, he saw this as a drama and the setting the same as that of act one.

Jay was prompt. He appeared before them, led by an employee of the club. Laurence and Kate both stood. "I'm Jay Smith," the man said, before the other two could gather their wits. He was over seventy—Kate had already figured that out—but clearly vigorous, standing quite straight. He bowed slightly toward her before sitting down.

"I'm Kate," Kate said. "Obviously," she continued, though why obviously she didn't quite know. True, she was the only woman present, but she might have been another relative sitting in for Kate, either because Kate had funked it or had asked someone else look this stranger over. Pull yourself together, Kate told herself.

But indeed, who she was, and who he was, was obvious because of the resemblance. Like Kate, he was tall and on the slim side, though like her now without the slimness of youth. Later, Reed would find the resemblance startling, though perhaps, he thought, only to someone looking for it, or to a portraitist. Jay's eyes were the same greenish gray as hers (why, Kate thought, have we never wondered why I am the only one in the family without blue eyes?) and both their two front upper teeth crossed slightly one upon the other. No wonder Laurence had not immediately sent the man packing.

A memory flashed across Kate's mind of a college friend who had confessed to an affair and subsequent doubt as to the father of her expected child. Anyway, she had startled Kate by saying, it hardly matters; the husband and the lover have the same coloring and the same eyes. Such a thought had clearly not occurred to Kate's mother. But then, she had probably had no doubt about who the father was, or the child's likely failure to resemble her husband in the slightest. Men like Fansler, as she would have known, took their wives' fidelity for granted; no doubt he attributed Kate's dissimilarity to her brothers either as the result of recessive genes exhibiting themselves, or, more probably, to the fact of her being a girl.

These thoughts, though rapid, had taken a little time. Kate realized they were all standing, and she sat, as did the other two. Laurence waved for a server. Kate asked for Scotch, as did Laurence. They both turned to Jay.

"Might I have tea?" he asked.

"Tea it is," Laurence said. "Tea for you, Kate, or will you stick to Scotch with me?"

"Scotch, please," she said. Some old-time family loyalty seemed called for. "Do you not drink," she asked Jay, "or only not in the afternoons?"

Aware that this was an impertinent inquiry, Kate shrugged to herself and waited to see how he would answer the question.

"I don't drink," he said. "A matter neither of principle nor addiction. I simply don't care for it."

"Fair enough," Kate said. A tea-drinker for a father; well, the resemblance was hardly likely to cover all elements. But she did feel disappointed, which was ridiculous.

"May I tell you the reason for my dislike, or what may be the reason?" Jay asked.

"Please do," Kate said, certain this promised to be the most bizarre conversation she had ever had in a life hardly devoid of oddball conversations.

"My mother was an alcoholic. As is not uncommon with the children of such parents, I came to loathe the smell of drink. Even wine, I'm afraid. I haven't, however, become a fighter for temperance

31

or an advocate of prohibition. Liquor doesn't bother me now when others drink it, and hasn't for a long time; I just don't wish to join in. You, may I guess," he said, smiling at Kate, "are of quite the opposite view, finding drink a happy companion to food and good conversation. I wish I could join you in that."

And, Kate thought to herself, I shall tell Reed that we began by speaking of drink. Jay's mother drank. Perhaps he was attracted to my mother because she didn't; it wasn't, of course, ladylike then, except for the careful sip of wine with dinner, and I don't even remember her doing that. Another unsummoned memory; this could become tedious.

Laurence seemed to feel that such an odd subject—even if Kate, in his opinion, always seemed to have peculiar conversations—needed some alteration.

"Kate is a professor; teaches literature. What do you do, Jay?" Thus Laurence commanded the dialogue onto another plane.

"I'm an architect; I specialize in the reconstruction of landmarks and other beautiful aging buildings. To combine modern convenience with the elegance of an earlier time is a challenge I find exciting."

"Can you really make a decent living doing that?" Laurence asked. Kate stared at him, only just remembering that when Laurence was nervous in a family situation, he was likely to say something downright rude, though he didn't realize it.

Jay looked unabashed. "A decent living, yes," he said, as his tea arrived, and he put sugar into the cup and stirred. Kate, who seemed currently given to unexpected recollections, recalled having been told that nondrinkers liked sugar, while drinkers, who often didn't, found their sugar in liquor. "But not a lavish one," he added. "No one, you see, is reliant on me for financial support, so I can do what I love to do—a great blessing."

This, the man's second private revelation, woke Kate to the fact that he might feel as though he were being interviewed, judged whether or not he was qualified for a position he did, after all, already occupy. She turned the conversation around to a comparison of architecture and literature, made easier for her by the fact that architecture had become a popular subject in academic literary departments. When it became clear that no other provocative matters were to be discussed, Laurence announced his intention to leave. It was, however, evident that he had not the smallest intention of retreating while they were still there. And so, shortly, they all stood up, ready to depart. While they were claiming their coats downstairs, Kate and Jay managed unobtrusively to exchange telephone numbers.

Outside on the street, Kate and Laurence shook Jay's hand. Laurence insisted upon seeing Kate into a taxi; the meeting must not continue without him. And so, with a moment of meaningful eye contact, Kate and Jay Ebenezer—for she could not quite yet think of him as her father—parted.

. . . thee my daughter who art ignorant of what thou art, naught knowing of whence I am.

Four

KATE CALLED JAY on the following day. She had, after some thought, decided that it was up to her to make the next move; reaching him by telephone, she suggested dinner in a quiet restaurant.

"Lovely," Jay said. "I'd like that. Soon. For now, what would you say to a walk in the park tomorrow? It's supposed to be a breezy March day; I've always liked breezy March days. We can just stroll about."

"Might I bring my dog?" Kate asked. "She's a rather large dog, but perfectly calm, either indifferent to overtures or casually friendly."

"Sounds the perfect companion to conversation. May I meet you on your corner whenever you say?"

"How about two?" Kate said. On this Friday, as on most, she had some sort of meeting in the morning, but would be free by two.

"Two it is," he said. Kate gave him her address and the location of the nearest corner.

"We're going to meet a new member of the family," she told Banny, who, deciding an immediate excursion was not being offered, stayed where she was.

For once, the weather forecast had been accurate: it was cool and breezy, with a feeling of spring in the air. Banny stood still to be greeted by Jay, but then looked at Kate, reminding her that the park had been promised. They crossed the street and set off around the lake. As they walked, they talked, but only intermittently. It occurred to Kate that in a restaurant they could have gazed at each other; strolling side by side, their words carried more meaning than their expressions or their appearance. Not a bad way to become acquainted, Kate thought.

In fact, their walk began in silence. Theirs was not a situation for which conventional or even mildly suitable dialogue had been established. Everything Kate wanted to ask she dismissed as outrageous even before it could be expressed. "How did you and my mother become lovers? How often did you sleep with each other? How, in sum, did it all come about?"

He seemed to sense her perplexity through her silence. "Ask anything you want," he said. "Or would you rather I began? I want to know so much about you."

"Perhaps we can take it by turns," Kate said, smiling. She would have liked to add that what he wanted to know about her fit more readily into the bounds of ordinary conversation than what she wanted to know about him. "I'll start. How old were you when . . . ?" She had been going to say when I was born, but she

35

really wanted to know about the nine months before that.

He understood her question. "I was not yet twenty when I met your mother. She was thirty-six. We became lovers soon after we met. It was the love of my life, and, I suspect, of hers. Sorry to sound so like a romance novel, but it does happen sometimes; I can testify to that."

Kate smiled at him. "Did you ever see the Noël Coward movie called *Brief Encounter*? I saw it on television not too long ago. It was the essence of impossible, perfect love, to the accompaniment of Rachmaninov's second piano concerto. When they part, the man says to the woman: 'I will love you all my life.' Is that the sort of thing?"

"I'm afraid it is. I adored her, and she was, I think, actually in love for the first time."

"Meaning, among other things, that she enjoyed sex for the first time?" Kate said, determined to be disgraceful and even scandalous. It was all very well, fathers turning up when one was getting along in one's fifties, but they could hardly carry on as though this were a play by Noël Coward, however much the endurance of original passion in that play testified to Coward's dramatic flair.

"Oh, yes," he said, unperturbed. "You are the child of passionate love. They used to say that made a person special, but I doubt it's true."

"I doubt it, too. It's more likely to make a person illegitimate," Kate said. "Fortunately, you two were hedged about by custom, and the Fansler talent for noticing nothing even under their noses until and unless it exploded. As it has now done."

They had, by this time, turned at the edge of the

lake, but instead of following the lake, they headed east for the boat pond. It was too early for children's sailboats, or the more complicated toy vessels driven by radio controls; the pond was drained. They sat on a bench, contemplating the passing scene; Banny lay down. The sun was in their faces, which they both found pleasurable.

Jay took her hand and held it for a moment, forcing her to look at him. "We both have questions; yours are about the past, and however personal, I intend to answer them honestly because you have the right to ask. My questions will be about the present: what you are now, what you think now, how you got there (some past allowed in this connection), where you expect or hope to be going. My questions will sound interested, which they are; yours may seem to sound probing, even audacious. You must ask them anyway; I really do see that, and hope you agree to this assessment of our different roles."

"I agree perfectly," Kate said. He let go of her hand, and they both again faced outward toward the pond. "So I'll begin, if only to say tell me about it, from the beginning. From when you met, and how. I've been trying to remember her, my mother. She's rather vague in my mind, probably because she was inclined to be offhand with me, apart from seeing that I was taught correct behavior, sent to good schools, dressed properly and never left to the mercy of my brothers—all of which seemed very much in the ordinary way of things. Had I been asked, and of course I wasn't, I would have said that she was indifferent to me, beyond her familial obligations. You mustn't think I minded. That was how mothers were expected to be, in those circles, in those years. The terrible fifties were really terrible."

"I suspect she was afraid of showing too much preference for you. True, you were a girl and therefore could be treated differently from the boys, but she feared to cast suspicion on your birth; your difference from your brothers seemed so obvious to her."

"It just occurs to me," Kate said. "She must have given my father reason to think I could have been his. Were they sleeping together then, my father and mother?"

"Oh, yes. He still made his marital demands with regularity; there was no problem on that score."

"Oh, the hell with the details," Kate said. Her imagination temporarily balked at contemplating the situation. "I just want to know how she acted in love; how it was with the two of you. I want to know she had that happiness, even for a while. I can't sound more like a soap opera than that, surely."

"She was happy with me," Jay said, "but she never would consider leaving Fansler for an uncertain, less endowed life with me. We parted finally a short while after you were born. I guessed, and I think I was correct, that she waited to see if you would be accepted as Fansler's child, with no questions asked by anyone. Once that was certain—and she appeared so proper, so firmly in her rather stiff role as wife and mother of Fanslers, that suspicion was unlikely. I departed soon after. She asked me not to try to get in touch with her again, and I consented. And here, half a century later, we are."

They sat for a time in silence, glancing at one another and smiling, as though admitting their curiosity and recognition of this strange meeting. Kate perceived, as she assumed Jay did, that there was a quality of flirtation about their reunion; he was an attractive man, clearly vigorous over the verge of seventy, and she, well, it hardly took much imagination to envision the whole business as a popular drama, a combination of drawing-room comedy and Eugene O'Neill, or as a soap opera.

Jay chuckled; he seemed to have followed her thought. "You mentioned soap operas a while back," he said. "That's not so far afield from where I began this attempt to find you and meet you. It was all the talk about DNA on police dramas, like *Law and Order*. I had thought often of looking you up, trying to get acquainted with you, but why should you believe that I was your father? Then the idea of DNA suddenly hit me: I can prove I'm her father, I suddenly realized. Why not do it then? DNA has released criminals from wrong convictions and imprisonment, why shouldn't it provide me with a daughter?"

"Why not, I guess," Kate said.

"You don't mind then?"

"I don't mind now. How could one mind such a luscious piece of drama entering one's life? If I had been asked did I want to find my 'real' father, would I have leapt eagerly to welcome the possibility? I'm not so sure."

"Well, here we are."

"Indeed. Are there questions you wish to ask me?" Kate said. "I have been doing all the quizzing."

"I know a good deal about you, as far as the facts go. Your career isn't hard to trace. You haven't any children?"

"No. Have you other children?"

"No. I married a woman with two sons; she was a widow, and I have been a father to them, as I think they would acknowledge. I adopted them. But they do not have my DNA."

"And how much does that matter?" Kate said. "I've been asking myself that ever since the news of you was delivered by poor, shocked, but fascinated Laurence. What made you go to him as your first move?"

"I thought it all out. It seemed the best way. You could always just refuse to see me without actually having to reject me personally."

"Most considerate. But you guessed that one can never keep from investigating a mystery about oneself."

"Hoped, rather. You are hardly the woman to act as expected. I'm glad you agreed to meet me."

"Any other questions for me now?" Kate asked.

"Only to ask if we might meet again. It's only logical that you would have more questions for me."

Kate nodded in agreement. "The matter of money, for instance. You told Laurence you wanted to find me in order to leave me money. I take it that wasn't the whole reason."

"It wasn't even part of the reason. That was an untruth, I'm afraid. Oh, I have some money to leave, but I'll probably will it to the boys, unless you have any thoughts on the subject. I . . . well, you see, I did rather know the Fansler outlook on life. I thought if I said I had money to leave, Laurence wouldn't think I was after your money or his. Sorry to have been deceptive, but it wasn't hard to figure out that you didn't need my money, so it wasn't likely you'd be disappointed not to get it."

"You don't hold a very high opinion of the Fanslers, do you?" Kate asked.

"Do you?"

"Not really. We don't agree on anything much, politics mainly, but almost everything else as well. Still, they are one's family. Or were. You make me wonder if my mother was ever really a Fansler."

"She chose to be one. She chose them over me."

"Do you think it was that she wanted to be well-off?"

"In part. She didn't have illusions about love keeping one warm, as the song went. But there was more to it than that; much more. There were her three sons, and your future, which was certainly better assured under Fansler auspices. And I think she felt she owed some loyalty to your father. Finally—and I spent a long time puzzling this out, as you can imagine—I think she felt herself suited to the Fansler life. I helped her to see that; there's the ironic part. Instead of feeling there would never be passion in her life, now there had been passion in her life. That had happened. She could go on as before, but having experienced something important."

"You make it sound rather cold-blooded, hard-hearted, logical."

"It was. I don't think that she was a romantic any more than you are. I've often wondered why she became pregnant; she had been in charge of the birth control. This is all the outcome of years of thought, but I decided that she had decided to give fate a chance. If there was a child, then what? If her husband would accept the child, that would be one

41

way fate might go; if he didn't, that would be another. I don't think she was so much logical as indulging in a form of Russian roulette. And having gone for the gamble, she stuck by the odds; she accepted the outcome."

"Shall we walk?" Kate asked. They rose and retraced their steps toward the lake, to Banny's evident relief; they had sat a good while.

"I think it's the whole question of DNA that keeps troubling me," Kate said. "Why should it make such a difference to us, discovering our relationship this late in both our lives. The truth is Reed has probably had more effect on me than your DNA has had; don't you think that's likely?"

"Yes, I do. And I hope to meet Reed one day soon, if you'll allow it. DNA was just the means of finding you, and of proving to you that I was your father. It wasn't a reason for anything. On the other hand, I may have wanted to find you because you're my only biological child. And—don't underestimate this—my only daughter."

There were swans on the lake. Central Park swans did not migrate to the south in the winter, apparently having, like Canadian geese, discovered ample supplies of food year-round in New York City. Soon the swans would be building a nest, as they did each year, on an island in the lake. Swans married for life, but went through the same courting rituals each year before mating. Kate had read up on swans since she had begun watching them on the Central Park lake, which was ever since she had had Banny to walk with.

She mentioned this casually to Jay, wanting to turn the conversation away from their quizzing of one another. And yet, she felt impelled to return to her questioning.

"I keep wondering about my mother," she said. "How it happened. It's always hard, I guess, to imagine one's mother in the throes of passion."

"As I told you at Laurence's club, my mother drank. My parents started out with promise, but there was the Depression, my father lost his job soon after I was born, it all went downhill. I think now, looking back, that my mother would have liked to have had a professional life, but that wasn't widely thought of for women in those years. She was depressed, she drank, my father lapsed into silence."

"Did your mother and father both like Dickens?"

"Ah, the Ebenezer connection. Yes indeed. They read to each other when they were first married; my mother told me that. And I was born on Christmas."

"That was Reed's guess," Kate said.

"When I met your mother, she was almost twenty years older than I. That doesn't seem much to me now, but it was that difference that made her so appealing to me. She seemed a finished woman, a complete woman, and a desirable one, the sort of woman I had never known. There was an immediate, powerful attraction between us. The truth is that at first she would have—what is the phrase?—thrown her hat over the windmill. She wanted to be outrageous, to risk being caught, to take awful chances. I was the sober one. Yet, in the end, it was she who made the sober decision. I guess I've always been a little bitter about it, though less so as the years went on."

"And meeting me has allowed for a measure of

revenge." Kate smiled, but they both knew there was truth in her words.

"I hope it allows for much more than that," Jay said.

"Time will tell," Kate said. "Reed and I will invite you to dinner—in a restaurant, we don't cook or entertain much—and we'll go on from there. One never knows what tomorrow will hold. As you can see, I conclude with clichés; it seems the soundest way to part this first time. I've just forgotten to ask one thing, which was how you met?"

"At a wedding, properly enough. I was the best man of the groom; we'd been at college together. There was dancing, of course. We danced. I saw her across the crowded room, just as the song says."

"As I said, we must part now in the midst of clichés."

And so, with plans to meet soon again, they went their separate ways.

The wide and universal theatre
Presents more woeful pageants
than the scene
Wherein we play in.

Five

A FEW DAYS later, Kate and Reed had dinner with Jay. As though by mutual agreement, although Kate and Reed had made no plans about their dinner conversation, they spoke of general matters—politics, food, architecture, the academic life, the law. The whole encounter went very pleasantly. Kate enjoyed leaving most of the conversation to the two men; it suited her, upon occasion, to play the quiet, unassertive woman, pleased to be in the company of two such intelligent and attractive men. She glanced from one to the other, smiling and nodding as, in courtesy, they turned to her. Toward the end of the meal, as they lingered over coffee, Kate was surprised by the fleeting impression that Reed was asking more, probing for more than the answers to the subjects under discussion. She knew him well enough to sense this, but then dismissed it as a fancy; it was certainly far from obvious. After all, one did not expect to meet one's father for the first time in one's fifties; it was only natural that everything should appear slightly askew. As they prepared to go their separate ways, they agreed to meet again shortly, and their parting was gracious, with Reed quite his usual self, courteous as ever. Kate decided she had been imagining things.

The next evening, however, she was forced to revert to her original impression. She and Reed were in their living room, having their usual predinner drink, when Reed, at a pause in the conversation about the the events of the day in politics and in their own lives, suddenly said:

"I love you, Kate."

The statement seemed unconnected with anything that had preceded it, and odd besides; Reed was not given to declarations of devotion. Kate stared at him.

"What?" she said.

"I love you. I just thought I would mention it."

"Reed, are you having an affair?"

"It's a great world we live in," Reed said, "where if a man tells his wife he loves her, she immediately assumes he's having an affair."

"He usually is. Though more usually, he tells her that on the telephone on his way to visit the other woman."

"I never knew you were so cheaply cynical, Kate."

"I never knew you went in for sudden assurances of marital love. One does rather take these things for granted, which is perhaps regrettable, but I can't help feeling there was a purpose in those words. All three of them."

"Clever you. There was a purpose, but you mistake its origins. I meant to speak of your father, and I wanted you to know I did so out of my love for you. I'm sure I could have put it better."

"What about my father? Since we now know him, might we call him Jay? It seems more suitable."

"Jay then."

"What about him?"

"You do realize, dear Kate, that we know nothing whatever about him, except that DNA has proved him to be your father. We were so intrigued with the demonstration of that fact, that we neglected to ask any other questions."

"I asked quite a few during our walk in the park, and very pointed ones at that."

"Yes, I know. But they were, were they not, questions about your mother, how they met, why they parted, that sort of thing? I don't doubt that he loved your mother, or at least fathered a child with her. What else do we know for certain?"

"He's an architect; he plans the restoration of old buildings; he's been married and has two adopted sons. He hasn't a lot of money though he claimed to have, to persuade Laurence that money wasn't his motive in wanting to meet me. I'm sure there's more, but that's quite a lot, isn't it?"

"What was his motive in wanting to meet you?"

"You don't consider finding a long-lost daughter sufficient motive?"

"It may be sufficient, or it may not. Why wait all this time?"

"He's past seventy. People do look back and try to tie up loose ends at that age, surely. Why does anyone do what they do when they do it and not at another time? What are you getting at, Reed?"

"That I'd like your permission to investigate him further. You may be right about him; he may be exactly who he says he is. But I'd like to have a look, all the same. I don't want to do it unless you agree it's sensible, and understand that love for you is my chief motive."

Kate laughed. "I think you're jealous of a man who's turned up as my father, and whatever you doubt you don't doubt that. Reed, I'm really moved to know that you feel that way. I used to have no relation in the world but you; I can hardly count the Fansler brothers, as you know. Now I have a father as well as a husband, and you seem to mind."

"Perhaps I do. Perhaps this is all the most errant nonsense, and cover for my nose being out of joint. But will you humor me all the same?"

"It does seem a bit like going behind his back, sneaking—not quite aboveboard or honest."

"True, but I shall be discreet. And if he gets word of my inquiries, I'll simply say that as your husband I felt the need to protect you. Of course, I wouldn't say or do any of this if you object."

"My impulse is not to object, but to insist that I know nothing about it."

"That doesn't sound like you."

"Oh, dear. Being discovered by one's father seems exciting at first, but perhaps it's more burdensome than I realized. All right; but don't go too far. If your first investigations pan out, just let it go, will you?"

"Let's put it this way. I'll let you know whatever I discover, and we can decide what I do next."

"Or what we do next."

"You're the detective, Kate, deny it as you will.

By now I think you can claim the title, even if you're never paid for your work. You may want to take over at any moment."

"Or not."

"Or not."

And they dropped that subject; Reed fixed them another drink before they moved to the kitchen and the preparations for dinner. But Kate had great difficulty getting Reed's suspicions out of her mind; she had to admit, in honesty, that she rather wished he hadn't had them. On the other hand, would they not, in time, have occurred to her?

Still brooding on this, she finally decided, later that night, to return to the subject of possible detective work about Jay, his past and, if it came to that, his present. She walked from her study to Reed's and stood in the doorway, waiting for him to look up.

"Come in," he said. "Don't lurk there as though you were plotting a quick escape."

Kate walked into the room and plopped down in Reed's large leather chair. He swirled toward her from his desk.

"I *was* plotting a quick escape," Kate said. "I just wanted to offer a suggestion."

"Suggest away."

"About Jay, you know."

"I had guessed."

"Yes. Well, instead of donning your detective cloak and galloping off down various investigative trails, why don't you just have lunch with him?"

Reed smiled. "Tell me about your life, I'll say. Start at the beginning and go on till you get to the end—which is this very moment. Is that what you had in mind?"

49

"More or less. Either he'll give you the truth, or most of it, or he'll refuse, or what he gives you won't be the truth. It seems to me that puts you further ahead in your search than you might be without the lunch."

"Right you are," Reed said. "Why didn't I think of that?"

"Meaning you had thought of it, I suppose."

"Only just, I admit. And I wasn't sure you'd like me playing the detective at lunch on your behalf. So I'm glad you mentioned it."

"I rather like the reversal," Kate said. "The husband asking the father what his intentions are."

"I was worried you might look at it in that light. Why don't you have the lunch?"

"I'd rather you would, Reed. Don't ask me why; I seem to want you to get some facts about the man in order before I continue the relationship. Besides, you're a lawyer, an ex-D.A., you're used to asking sharp questions. I dislike personal questions, at least direct ones. Oh, hell, I'm just putting it off on to you. Should I be the one?"

"No; I'll be glad to cross-examine the guy. Perhaps I'll feel better about this whole thing."

"I didn't know it bothered you."

"I didn't either. When it began to bother me, I told you about it right away."

"That's settled then," Kate said. "Give the man a call and set up a leisurely lunch."

Reed and Jay met the next day in the Oak Room of the Plaza for lunch. Reed was following Kate's rather joking proposal that they meet in the Oak Room since that was where she had wanted to meet

Jay in the first place. She had, on that occasion, been denied the Oak Room, given Laurence's insistence that they meet at his club. Reed now saw no reason not to follow Kate's suggestion, and therefore found himself in the Oak Room, across from Jay, studying the menu, with less idea of what he was going to say than of what he wanted to eat.

"Whatever you have on draft," he said. "Or, if you have nothing on draft, anything at all."

Reed had, of course, undertaken many conversations with lawyers, criminals, and students, and had no difficulty with opening remarks or with asking for what he wanted. Still, these skirmishes—one could hardly call them conversations; there were occasionally altercations—had not taken place in such elegant surroundings nor on a subject concerning his wife. Jay guessed at the reasons for Reed's hesitation, his head buried in the menu.

"I know what I want to eat," Jay said, "and I suspect I know what you want to talk about: my intentions toward your wife. Am I right?"

"Not exactly," Reed said, deciding on his meal. The waiter appeared to take their orders and reclaim their menus. Jay broke open a roll and buttered it. Then he put it down and reached into the inside pocket of his jacket. He handed the folded paper to Reed.

"That's my résumé," he said. "From 1950 on, all my jobs more or less, though I haven't gone into details. In fact, I can't remember all the names exactly. Also, there are a few lacunae when I was in between jobs or between temporary ones, but on the whole it's a pretty complete picture. That's what you wanted to know, isn't it?"

Reed unfolded the sheet of paper and examined it. "Fortunately you're not a lawyer," he said. "When one is admitted to the bar, it is necessary to list every job one has ever had, including summer and temporary ones."

"It's different with architecture. Either you're working at it, or at something else until you can work at it again."

"I gather it's a rather volatile profession."

"Exactly like the stock market, which is a good barometer of architecture's fortunes. When times are good, people build or, in my case, restore. When there's a recession, building and restoration are among the first things to be postponed."

As their drinks arrived, followed by their food, Reed continued to glance at the paper. "Do you mind if I ask a few questions as I read along?" he asked.

"Not at all." Jay began on his salad and then chuckled. Reed looked up. "I was thinking of my wife," Jay said. "She used to ask me what men talked about when they were alone. She seemed to think we spent our time together telling male jokes and slandering women. I was hard put to convince her that the men I knew usually had something particular to discuss and simply got on with it."

"No doubt there are other kinds of male conversations."

"Of course. But my wife seemed to think there was only one kind, portrayed on television by men in bars. I need hardly add that she was nothing like Kate."

"Or Kate's mother?"

"The resemblance was closer there, but not very

close. My wife didn't have a profession nor want one."

Reed nodded and went on with his reading. "When did you leave Kate's mother?" he asked, putting the paper temporarily aside.

"Not long after Kate was born; a few months later. I urged her to come away with me, bringing our baby, but she refused. Fansler had indicated no doubts about Kate's paternity. She wanted to stay with him."

"So you went west," Reed said, glancing at the résumé, now at the side of his plate.

"Yes. I was avoiding the temptation to return to her, to visit. Three thousand miles seemed a sensible distance at the time; anyway, it was the farthest away I could get."

"Did you help to decide on the baby's, on Kate's name?"

"Oh, yes. It was Shakespeare's favorite woman's name. Rosalind was, and is, my favorite woman character in Shakespeare, but Louise would not agree on Rosalind, so Kate it was. Louise wanted Katherine, but I stood my ground."

"Fansler had nothing to say on the matter?"

"No. He had named the sons; he considered the daughter's name her mother's choice."

"An old-fashioned, conventional family."

"Surely," Jay smiled, " 'There needs no ghost, my lord, come from the grave to tell us this.' To tell you, that is."

"Kate shares your passion for Shakespeare."

"But it's not what she teaches."

"Not since her first teaching days." Reed refused to let the conversation revert to Kate. "Did you know you would work as an architect when you went west? That seems to have come later."

"I was studying architecture when I met Louise. I returned to it some years later."

"So I see; you studied architecture at Yale."

"Yes. But I eventually met up with a chap from Columbia, and we started our firm."

"But not in New York."

"No. I never returned to New York to work, except for the occasional project. By the time the west woke up to the fact that they ought to preserve a few of their older buildings—and by this time the bulldozers had knocked most of them down—there was a good bit of work for us out there."

"You came back to New Haven, but you never visited the Fanslers or Louise or Kate."

"No. I had promised not to; I kept my promise until a few weeks ago. Everyone who might have given a damn was dead."

"What about your adopted sons?"

"We don't meet often. I may tell them one of these days. I suspect they'll be glad to hear I was such a randy fellow in my youth."

"I never knew Kate's parents," Reed said. "They were dead before I met her; they both died on the young side."

Reed had, more than once, heard from Kate how conventional her mother was, insisting that Kate go to dancing school and behave in a manner appropriate to the mother's ideas of ladylike behavior. Reed had often wondered what would have happened if Louise had lived past sixty, long enough to face the fact that Kate was determined to be a professional, a feminist and a far from ladylike woman.

Louise had become ill some years before her death, and had not challenged Kate, nor disputed with her. Reed wondered now if perhaps it was not her illness, but her memories of Kate's father that explained her tolerance of Kate's decisions.

He did not mention this. "What sort of temporary work did you undertake when you weren't being an architect?" he asked.

"Subcontracting, usually, or just working as a builder. I liked learning how one put up buildings, or how to renovate them; it was work I could almost always get. In good times, workers with experience were needed; in bad times, workers who came cheap were desired. That was how it went, during most of the between periods."

Reed could think of nothing else to ask. In fact, he could think of much else to ask, but this hardly seemed the time or place for such questions; some of them could never be asked. As to the résumé, he needed to study it more closely, and perhaps make a few inquiries.

"You've been most agreeable about all this," he said to Jay. "You might well have told me to stuff it."

"I'm glad you wanted to know more about me. I'm glad Kate's married to someone who cared to find out more about her father."

"I wouldn't have even met with you unless Kate agreed," Reed said.

"I took that for granted."

Reed smiled, and reached for his wallet.

"Do let me pay," Jay said. "I've been the cause of all this inquiry."

"Another time," Reed said.

Do you not know I am a
woman?
When I think I must speak.

Six

REED HANDED JAY'S résumé to Kate.

"He gave it to you?" she asked, glancing at it. "It's all typed up. You mean he brought it to you unasked?"

"All of those," Reed said. "He's no fool; he guessed why I wanted to see him. This was to show me how he'd spent his life and that he was as open as anyone could be."

"A busy life," Kate said, reading the résumé. "He worked as an architect or builder most of the time; just as he told us. Is his architecture firm still in existence?"

"Oh, yes. See, he gives the address, the phone numbers, the name of his partner who now runs it. All clean and aboveboard."

"Why do I catch a note of skepticism? I take it the lunch did nothing to assuage your doubts about him."

"Look at that résumé more carefully."

Kate studied it in detail, pausing over each entry. "There are lacunae, of course. And whatever it was he was doing seems a little vague after he went west, but is that so unexpected? And doesn't everyone have gaps unless they're trying to be appointed as a judge or attorney general?"

"He explained the gaps to some extent. In between jobs in restoration he worked temporarily as a subcontractor, a carpenter, a bricklayer possibly. That's not what's troubling me. Look at the years between 1970 and 1975."

"I see," Kate said. "Nothing much there. Perhaps we are to assume that it was temporary jobs again."

"Why not say so?"

Kate smiled. "I don't remember you being this serious before, this doubtful. Is there something about Jay that's getting to you? Aside from the fact that he's my father."

"That's rather a bigger aside than usual. Perhaps I'm jealous of this new man in your life; perhaps I'm just naturally a mean, suspicious person. I can't really tell you why, but I sense something not quite right. It need not be something to his discredit; it may merely be something he'd rather not disclose. If you don't want me to snoop, just say so."

"Of course you must snoop as you choose, provided you keep me informed of all you uncover." Kate grinned at him. "But as you keep telling me, whatever he had to offer me in the way of a paternal inheritance he's already done. Nothing we can find out will change that."

"Kate," Reed said, answering the undertone rather than her words. "If you have the slightest hesitation about my looking further into the life of Jay Ebenezer

Smith, just say so. As you so wisely point out, there's nothing to be learned that could affect you in any way."

"Do you think the name is made up too? It does sound a bit unlikely."

"Only because Smith is so common a name that, if we suspect someone of dishonesty who says his name is Smith, we tend to assume he's lying."

"That is not a logical sentence," Kate said.

"No, but it's a logical thought which, as usual, I trust you to disentangle from my sorry syntax."

They were again in Reed's study, where Kate had found him on her return from the university. She fully extended his lounge chair and lay in it quietly for some minutes. Reed, behind his desk where he had been working, watched her. One of his most prized qualities, in Kate's view, was that he could look at her and wait to hear her response, not, as with so many of the males she encountered, waiting to speak themselves, or retreating into their own private musings.

"I can't decide if I want to know more about him or not," she eventually said, having tried to sort out her thoughts. "I want to go on seeing him from time to time, to stay in touch. I'll certainly be interested, not to say engrossed, in anything I learn about him. But whether or not I think we, you, ought to dig into his past is a different question. We both realize, I hope, that those missing years will turn out to have been a series of jobs so repetitive and dull that he saw no point in reporting them; probably he couldn't even remember them all."

"Probably," Reed said.

"But if I agree, you'd still like to dig a little?"

"I think so."

"Well," Kate said, pulling herself and the lounge chair into an upright position, "I can't imagine how you'd even begin, but if begin you must, you have my agreement, if not quite my blessing. I've never investigated the past, exactly. I'll learn a lot watching how you do it."

"You're already beginning to discourage me," Reed said. "But not definitively."

The next day, a Friday, Kate went in the afternoon to talk with her friend Leslie Stewart, who was a painter and could be found in her studio, happy—if her guest was both expected and welcome—to put down her brush and relax. Between her and Kate there was likely to be brisk and enjoyable conversation. They went into the kitchen where, as was their habit, they drank tea, which Kate never did anywhere else, and nibbled on ginger cookies.

"I take it that acquiring a father this late in life is having disruptive effects?" Leslie said. "I don't wonder. Finding out in one's later middle years, as I did, that one is in love with a woman is certainly an astonishing experience, but this is even more noteworthy. And to think that without DNA he could have claimed fatherhood till the cows came home, and you would hardly have believed him. At least, you would never have known for sure and could have sent him packing."

"I hadn't thought of it that way," Kate said. "He was clever enough to prove he was my father before suggesting that we meet. One shudders to think what the world will be like in future years with all our genes mapped and if necessary altered, to say

59

nothing of giving away the secrets of the marriage bed."

"Or the hurly-burly of the chaise longue, as Shaw or someone put it. Did you want to discuss genes or your father?" Leslie asked. "I'm ready for either, though at the moment I find the latter more challenging."

"That's just it," Kate said. "I can't decide whether I think his turning up is challenging or, after the first shock, simply another fact to be calmly accepted. It's a romantic story, all right, and certainly casts my mother in a new light; but all that's the past. Does the fact of this man have any bearing on my future, or my peace of mind?"

"Maybe it depends what you think about fathers generally. They, after all, particularly for our generation and the women before us, are the carriers of the patriarchy, the male world, the sense of men as human beings and women as an interesting, if usually annoying, appendage. Does it matter who carries the disease?"

"It may matter whether the carrier—to continue your metaphor—is infecting one purposely, accidentally, or not at all."

"Good point, Kate. But surely whatever effect either father might have had, or did have on you, is hardly significant now. It's not as though some other woman had turned out to be your mother."

"That, I'm relieved to say, would have been impossible. After all, my brothers would have noticed if there had been a substitution."

"Anyway, of what importance were mothers in our day? If it comes to that, what is there to be said about the relationship between mothers and daughters at any time—speaking honestly, of course."

"I didn't have much of a relationship with my mother," Kate said. "But I did come to realize some years ago that she had permitted me, without hysterical confrontations or without confessing it, to live the life I wanted, or to prepare for the life I wanted. She died before she had to witness the results of her tolerance. And it was a tolerance cleverly camouflaged by her insistence on conventionality. Now that I know she had a lover, she returns to me in a new light, or at least from a new perspective. Perhaps that's the most important result of Jay's materializing at this late date."

"Your mother's dead; you can afford to be sentimental and ooze gratitude," Leslie said, pouring more tea. "Dead mothers are one thing. Living mothers—and remember, I'm one, as well as a daughter and an observant woman—are at best necessary supplements to life whom we tolerate, if we are kind, with courtesy and generosity. Remember, that's at best. More often than not there's a residue of resentment on both sides, and civility is barely maintained."

"Leslie, motherhood has never been your long suit in the game of life," Kate said, relishing the idiom or cliché, though she hadn't a clue what card game was providing the metaphor. "Anyway, I've acquired a father, not a mother."

"I will say for you, Kate, that you've never gone on about the emptiness in your life because you don't have children. I try to convince childless women of the advantages of their condition, but they just say since I have children I haven't a right to speak on the subject. That seems to me an idiotic objection there's no way out of. The truth is, Kate, you get more pleasure from your present and past graduate students, to say nothing of your niece and nephew, than most people, myself included, get from their children."

"I get pleasure only from some graduate students, and only from two of my many nieces and nephews," Kate said defensively. "And don't forget Benedict's defense: 'The world must be peopled.' "

"Not these days. With all this genetic work curing and preventing diseases, everyone will live forever, and we had better find a way not to people the world, and soon."

"Genes, again. You see, they do keep turning up. Now could we get back to my father?"

"Right," Leslie said. "Why not just enjoy it. Let all the ramifications of your genetic heritage whirl about in your brain, follow each supposition to its illogical but fascinating conclusion, and then just look on him as a new friend. That's my advice. You did come for my advice, didn't you."

"I came for the tea. Reed is suspicious of Jay. Not of his motives in turning up, but of his past, which Reed seems to suspect of being murky."

"Well, there's murky and murky. Promise not to spare me a single detail."

"What I can't decide," Kate said, "and I know I keep returning to this, is what difference it makes who was one's father. I mean, half a century later, what can Jay's appearance possibly mean?"

"Now that's an easy one. It obviously provides a simple, irrefutable explanation of why you aren't a standard Fansler. No one else in the family turned out even remotely interesting."

"No doubt. But am I really ready to believe—which I never had to do before—that it is only spermatozoa that made me what I am today."

"Probably. And yesterday, and all the days before that. Is the truth of your paternal heritage so disturbing, and if so, why?"

"I don't know," Kate said.

"I do. You have long prided yourself, with justification, on breaking away from every opportunity to be a self-satisfied, conventional, right-wing, wealthy, socially established Fansler. Now it turns out, you don't get any credit, or not much. It all goes to Jay—whom I insist upon meeting in the very near future."

"I might have had Jay for a father and still become a traditional Fansler. After all, that was my upbringing, my identity."

"I know that, you owl. I'm just teasing you. But I do think Jay's appearance has ever so slightly dented your amour propre."

Kate sighed. She was not about to admit to Leslie the stunning accuracy of her analysis, but she was beginning to acknowledge it to herself. "And what shall I do if my father turns out to have been something either illegal or shameful or maybe both?"

"If you're worried about it, I'd stop Reed from investigating. You'd have gone on with your life quite nicely, thank you, if your father had never darkened your door, but since he has, why not let well enough alone?"

"Good question, but I told Reed he could go ahead. I don't feel entitled, after the life I've led, to turn away from learning something just because it might turn out to be disturbing."

"You're right, of course. Now," Leslie said, "could I complain for a while? There is more that can be annoying in life than was ever dreamed of in your philosophy. Art galleries, for example."

And they went on to speak of Leslie's life.

But the question of how to think about Kate's father, or whether to investigate him, or whether his appearance affected Kate's view of herself—these questions vanished almost without a trace. Jay Ebenezer Smith disappeared as suddenly and as shockingly as he had materialized.

Seven

IT WAS SEVERAL days before Kate noticed that Jay had not called as promised, and that calls to him were not answered; nor was there any longer a machine to take messages. Well, she thought at first, anyone can be called out of town, or be faced with some unforeseen demand. But when a week beyond when he had said he would call her had gone by, she asked Reed if he thought she should look into the matter.

Reed found it odd that Jay had promised to call Kate and failed to do so. People often made empty promises, but surely if one had gone to so much trouble to look up a daughter one had not seen in half a century or more, one would not simply forget to make a promised telephone call. In the end Reed offered to go around to his apartment and see if he could learn anything about Jay's whereabouts. Kate said she would come, too.

Jay had told them that he had sublet a small

apartment in a large building near Astor Place; toward this they set off on a Saturday morning. Banny looked woeful at being left by both of them, but settled down, head on paws, to await their return.

"Meeting this man involves a certain amount of unaccustomed intracity travel," Kate observed. "First Laurence's club, then you off to the Plaza, now we move on to Astor Place."

They took the subway to West Fourth Street and walked eastward across town to the address Jay had given them. It turned out to be a large building indeed; in fact, it occupied a square block, and was guarded at the entrance by two men who demanded to know to whom they wished to be announced. Reed began by giving Jay's name in the usual way, but was hardly surprised when the house phone to his apartment failed to elicit a reply.

"Have you seen Mr. Smith lately?" Reed asked the doorman.

"Not lately, no," the man replied, as though he had just realized this. With as many apartments as this house contained, the doorman grumpily explained, he could hardly remember who came and went. But, it seemed, he could dredge up a memory of who had not come or gone. "It's a while since I've seen him, now that you ask," the man said. "Maybe a week; maybe less."

"Might we be able to look into his apartment?" Reed asked. "Just to be sure that he is not there; not, perhaps, ill or injured."

The doorman looked them over. Kate had the impression that were they, well, less proper looking, or younger, he might have simply refused. As it was, he agreed to call the superintendent, leaving the decision up to him. Kate wondered if Reed had plans beyond the legal way of getting into the apartment, and reminded herself to ask him later.

If Reed had nurtured more nefarious plans to gain entrance to Jay's apartment, he did not need them. The superintendent led them to the elevators, thence to one of many doors on a long corridor. He knocked loudly, waited, knocked again and called. Then he opened the door with his master key, still calling. There was no response; the apartment looked not only empty but deserted, though Kate would have been hard put to explain exactly in what this impression of abandonment consisted.

They followed the superintendent as he walked about the apartment, opening the doors to closets; all the other doors to the few rooms, even to the bathroom, stood open. It was what was usually called a three-room apartment: living room, bedroom, kitchen, bath. There was a small foyer, and a generous allotment of closets. The whole place was neat, as though it had been recently cleaned, although a light layer of dust on some of the furniture suggested that another cleaning was shortly due.

Even as they stood in the living room trying to decide what the apartment was telling them, if anything, there came a knock on the apartment door, which stood open. It was, evidently, the cleaning woman. She greeted the superintendent, and stared at Reed and Kate.

"Anything wrong?" she asked.

"I hope not, Maria," the super said. "These are friends of Mr. Smith's; it seems he hasn't been heard from these last few days. This"—the super turned to Reed and Kate—"is Maria. She cleans for several people in the building, and for the people from whom Mr. Smith sublet this apartment. When were you last here, Maria?"

"A week ago," she said. "I hope nothing's wrong with Mr. Smith."

"Probably nothing is," the super said. "He's probably had to go away suddenly and forgot to notify his friends."

"He always leaves me a note and my money," Maria said.

They looked again, but found no note, no money.

"Perhaps you had better come back another day, Maria," the super said.

"Before you go, Maria," Reed said, "would you be good enough to look around—the kitchen, the bathroom, everywhere—and tell us if you think anyone has been here since you last cleaned?"

Maria nodded and went to examine the rooms as she had been requested to do. The woman was Hispanic but spoke excellent English. Reed in his long legal career had met many like her. Clearly intelligent, she worked as a cleaning woman, but her children went to parochial schools and would go to college; they would never need to clean other people's homes. It was, in Reed's opinion, a not unusual, yet admirable and difficult immigrant story; it had a long history. The countries of origin changed, but not the hard work or the ambitions for the next generation.

Maria returned to report that no one had been here since her last visit. She could tell from the bathroom and kitchen, although nothing seemed to have been touched in the other rooms. Mr. Smith's bed was still made as she had made it a week ago;

he left it unmade for her to change the sheets. The kitchen was exactly as she had left it; the bathroom shower and towels had not been used.

They thanked Maria and, when she had left, asked the superintendent if they might look through Mr. Smith's drawers and closets for a clue as to where he might have gone. The super was reluctant to give this permission, but did, hovering over Reed as he opened drawers and closet doors. Nothing of the slightest significance emerged from this search. Nor was there anything worth noting in or on the desk: no address book, no date book, no computer. The closets contained only a minimum of clothes, supposedly Jay's. The contents of the linen closet and the kitchen cupboards obviously belonged to the apartment's owners. The only clue to be found was the blatant evidence that nothing of Jay's remained, no sign of him, no indications, apart from his few clothes, that he had ever been here.

"Did you meet Mr. Smith?" Reed asked the super.

"Oh, yes. I greeted him when he moved in. We only allow apartments to be sublet for brief periods, and under certain conditions. I always keep an eye on subtenants; there's rarely any trouble. He was a pleasant man." Which, Reed thought, probably meant that he was a good tipper and didn't complain about anything.

They left the apartment, the super carefully double-locking the door and then escorting them to the building's entrance. Clearly, life in this multiple dwelling was closely watched; there were monitors in the entrance hall, showing the elevators and all of the lobby not directly in the doorman's vision, allowing him to oversee all comings and goings.

Somehow, Kate admitted as they walked away, the place made her nervous. She supposed that if one lived there, one might get used to it. Maybe.

"Most of the tenants are probably older people who have moved back to the city from the suburbs, or from large city apartments," Reed said. "They value security above all else."

"Do you suppose Jay knew the people he rented the apartment from?" Kate asked.

"I doubt it. Though he must have been pretty thoroughly vetted. I think I'll get in touch with the building's management firm and see what information he gave them."

This additional inquiry, however, produced nothing of interest. Jay had given the name of the architecture firm with which he still maintained some connection, his bank, his broker. In addition, he had paid all the rent he would owe in advance, so there was no question of his defaulting.

"Do subletters always do that?" Kate asked that evening as they reviewed what information they had gathered—hardly new information at all.

"No. It's a bit unusual. Why pay in advance instead of letting the money accumulate interest in the bank or elsewhere? It almost seems as though he was preparing for a quick exit, if necessary."

"Which you think he has done—exited, I mean?"

"It looks that way. Of course, there may be a perfectly simple explanation. Time will tell." But from his tone, Kate rather doubted Reed believed this.

"Would you have broken into that apartment if we hadn't got in as we did?" Kate asked.

"I'd hardly have broken in," Reed said, smiling.

"But I would have managed to get in some way or other."

The question was: what to do next? Ought they to do anything?

Reed walked up and down the room, deep, Kate suspected, in the contemplation of various plots. "I don't like it, Kate," he finally said. "I haven't really liked it from the beginning; I admit that. To turn up as he did is odd enough, but then to disappear. If it weren't for the DNA evidence, I'd set the police after him."

"Or at least a private detective." She grinned at him.

"I think we just wait a few days and see if anything happens."

"And then?"

"We just wait."

Reed, however, while he was ostensibly waiting, got in touch with Yale's alumni office, asking to confirm that Jason Ebenezer Smith had been a student in the architecture school; he gave the years of attendance as Jay had included them on his résumé. The answer, when the alumni office called him back, hardly astonished him. There had been no one of that name in the class Reed had mentioned, nor in the preceding or following year.

Reed asked then if he might be sent a list of the members of Jay's supposed class. He explained that he was a professor of law, calling from the law school, and that he needed the information for an investigation he was pursuing; he would also be grateful for any information they had on the architectural firms with which members of that class were, or had been, associated—the sort of account got up for reunions. Reed promised that the list would not be used for fund-raising, or any other nefarious purpose. In the end, having gone off to consult with a higher authority, the person on the phone agreed to send Reed what he wanted. He could, after all, have got it from any number of sources or connections, and there seemed no reason to deny the request.

The information came through by fax an hour later. Reed pored over it with more eagerness than he would readily have admitted to Kate or anyone else. Two graduates of the class were associated with Jay's firm—at least with the firm Jay had claimed to have founded. Reed picked up the phone and called it; he asked for each man. He was told that one of them had had a stroke and retired to Florida; the other man was still a member of the firm, but no longer worked there full-time. He did come in often, however, although he was not in at present. Did Reed care to leave a message? Reed declined the offer, with thanks.

The no-longer full-time member of the firm was named Edmund M. Dyson. Unable to abandon the trail, Reed walked over to the library to consult a directory of architecture firms and architects. Edmund M. Dyson's career paralleled Jay's; indeed, it was in many respects identical to it, except that Jay had not mentioned all his honors in his résumé. This was perhaps modesty, or awareness that these awards offered too easy a clue to his other identity.

The unavoidable fact was that, by any name, he was Kate's father. But why the name change, why the subterfuge, why, if it came to that, look Kate up at all? He must have foreseen that doing so would lead to an investigation, and that his true identity would very soon emerge. Reed badly wanted to confront Jay, who had now disappeared, which was damn frustrating. All sorts of possible plots surged through Reed's mind, but none of them made any sense. He was a man who had wanted, late in life, to meet his daughter. Was the rest of any real importance? Could this be some racket after all, to do with money or some fraudulent scheme? Kate was hardly the natural object for such a maneuver, let alone the fact that she was married to a former assistant D.A. with contacts in the legal world, and was related to powerful figures in the investment world.

Still bristling with frustration, Reed set off for home. He would tell Kate what he had discovered. Protecting her was not part of their partnership, nor did he keep secrets from her for any reason, apart from professional matters that he did not discuss with her or anyone other than those directly concerned. The only question before him now was whether or not to persuade her to abandon the whole investigation into Jay's identity and life. Provided Jay did not return, provided there was no further news of him, might it not be more sensible to let the matter, at least for the present, rest?

He had about convinced himself that this was the better course of action. He had in fact decided to urge Kate to accept the wisdom of this advice, and had even begun to rehearse how he would present it to her. After all, he would point out, she had not particularly wanted to undertake the investigation of Jay in the first place. She had only gone along, and that reluctantly, with his impulse to find out more about her suddenly appearing father. So why should she argue with his recommendations about abandoning the search?

When he arrived home, however, Kate emerged from her study to greet him.

"What now?" he asked, rather irritably. When one has spent so much energy planning a conversation, one does not welcome having it diverted before it begins.

"I've had a short note from Jay," Kate said. "Scrawled on a piece of paper, and left with the doorman. I asked him, the doorman, about the man who left it, but he said a black man handed it to him. I doubt it was Jay in disguise."

"A messenger, obviously," Reed said. "What did Jay scrawl on the piece of paper?" Kate was holding it in her hand.

She looked at it, although she certainly knew what it said. She read it to Reed. "It says: 'Sorry to disappear. I'll be back in touch. Tell Reed it's not quite as bad as it looks.' " Kate glanced at Reed. "Do you think he knew you were planning to investigate him?"

"Of course he did," Reed said. "Damn it to hell." And having poured drinks for them both, he collapsed in the living room and told Kate all about that day's inquiries.

Kate sipped her drink and had a short exchange of pleasantries with Banny before responding to Reed's report.

"He changed his name. But he is an architect. And he did go to Yale. And he did take the time, and perhaps the risk, to let me know he'd gone. All
74

right, he's been one step ahead of us all the time, and you find it annoying. I don't blame you. I guess I've been more dazed than curious, more concerned with what effect, if any, the knowledge of him as my father makes in my life. Do you still want to go on probing?"

"Not for the moment," Reed said, draining his glass and extended his long legs their full length. He also raised his arms above his head and stretched them. "I think we might as well admit that the next move, if any, is his. But," he added, getting up to refill their glasses, "I don't promise not to think about it."

"And you'll keep me up on what you're thinking?"

"Absolutely, if I come up with anything more than meaningless, unescapable cogitation. You know, Kate, I think I'm getting to like Jay more than I originally did. No, don't ask me why. I haven't a clue."

Eight

AFTER HER INTRODUCTION to Jay which Laurence had arranged at his club, Kate had given no further thought to Laurence or her other brothers, nor had she wondered if they had been in any way disturbed by the revelation about their mother that Jay's appearance had forced upon them. Kate was so used to thinking of her brothers as conventional and conservative in the extreme, not to say boring—stultifying might better have described the effect of their conversation upon her—that she had failed to consider how the shock of Jay's appearance might have affected them. She and Reed no longer saw much of her brothers or their families; occasions to which it was felt that she and Reed must be invited were few. She was therefore considerably unnerved to hear the next day from all three of her outraged brothers. They had probably not planned to telephone in a series, one after the other within a few hours, but so it had turned out.

They had, she gathered, been working themselves up to confronting Kate, or at the least to informing her of their entire disapproval of this man who had so suddenly, and so irrefutably, appeared to cast aspersions on the reputation of their beloved mother. Now that the man had disappeared, as Kate, when asked, had been forced to admit to Laurence, they insisted upon a family conference. Kate did not doubt that they had been goaded to this by their wives, nor did she expect the wives to be included in this unpleasant gathering; Fansler wives were, in times of stress, attended to in private but were not permitted to be present in what were considered business meetings. Kate decided, however, that Reed would certainly be present; she did not intend to face her brothers alone—not in this case.

Reed pointed out to her that their feelings of violation, to say nothing of disgrace, were hardly to be condemned out of hand. Louise had been their mother as well as Kate's; no doubt they now considered her more their mother than Kate's; she had not behaved in so wildly appalling and unaccustomed a manner before their arrival in the Fansler family.

"Now, Reed," Kate said, responding with more irritation than she knew to be deserved, "there's no need to act as though we were all living in some earlier time—if there ever was an earlier time when bored and lonely women did not have lovers."

Reed did not take up this argument, which he doubted Kate even intended to pursue. "You must understand, dear Kate," he went on in a kindly manner certain to increase her irritation, "that their mother embodied their ideal of womanhood. No doubt they chose their wives because they assumed

77

them to resemble their mother in all important aspects."

" 'I want a gal just like the gal who married dear old dad,' " Kate sang, with something regrettably close to a sneer.

"She was their mother also," Reed repeated in a more conciliatory tone. "I think you should meet with them and offer them sympathy, pointing out your own state of shock and, incidentally, the fact that you had hardly planned for your biological father to turn up in that tumultuous way."

"He wasn't a bit tumultuous; he was as cautious as possible; even you noticed that."

"What on earth is the matter with you, Kate? I've never known you to be so intolerant and so impatient. Try to see it from their point of view."

"If you learned tomorrow that your mother had had an affair, even that your father wasn't your father, would you get your knickers in such a twist?"

Reed seemed to consider the question. "The truth is, I can't imagine such a possibility. But don't you see, that's just the point. Neither could they. And this new DNA technique doesn't offer them the chance to call Jay a liar and an impostor. The same method even proved Jefferson's congress with a slave, and he was one of the authors of the Declaration of Independence though a little less certain about the independence of slaves."

Kate abandoned her protests. "Say you'll come with me, Reed. Do you suppose we'll meet again at Laurence's club, or perhaps in the Oak Room?"

"If I know Laurence," Reed said, "we'll meet in his office, with the door shut. Laurence behind his desk, William and David in chairs side by side, and you and I on a couch opposite the three of them. You must promise me to listen, to sigh sympathetically, and to indicate in your looks as in your speech that you too are devastated by the thought of your mother's perfidy."

"Devastated? I think it's the best thing that ever happened to her, and it's made me happy to know she had it off with a good lover, at least for a time."

"*Kate!*" Reed was glowering. "I'm not accompanying you to that meeting unless you promise to behave as I have indicated."

"It's a promise," Kate said. "I'm certainly not facing those three alone, even if I have to pretend that adultery in women is far more serious a matter than a husband's fling."

"There is no need to exaggerate," Reed said.

They met the following afternoon, late, after Kate's class and office hour. She arrived alone. The men had all preceded her there, and rose at her entrance, though not without simultaneously glaring at her, the Fansler faces devoid of smiles. She was not offered any refreshment, and might have asked for something—surely a cup of tea would have been appropriate—but Reed glared in his turn, and she subsided on to the couch beside him. She could not, she realized, remember when she had last been in a room with all three of her brothers and no other Fansler. She regarded them now as though they were strangers to whom she had just been introduced. They wore suits with vests and somber ties, although their colored shirts would surely not have been thought suitable in earlier times. David even had a white collar on his blue shirt, quite dashing in its way. Kate had been tempted that morning to put on a skirt, but banished the thought; she wore trousers, with a silk blouse under an elegant jacket, and pearls. Well, one owed something to one's family, however prelapsarian. And then the pertinence of that word—for her mother had certainly had a "fall"—so pleased her that she smiled before quickly repressing it.

All this had been the matter of a minute at most. Laurence cleared his throat. "The question is," he announced, his opening words having, as was obvious, earlier been decided upon, "what are we going to do about this appalling situation?"

They all looked at Kate.

"Do?" she asked. "Is there anything to *do*?"

"We must try to keep it from the children," Laurence said. "I have not mentioned it to my wife, and have advised William and David to act likewise. The fewer who know, the better. We must avoid scandal at all costs."

Kate, who had been congratulating herself on the mildness of her intentions, let out an exclamation of amazement.

"*Scandal!* Laurence, what century are you living in? We've recently entered a new one, or didn't you notice? There hasn't been such a thing as scandal—politics aside—since 1970 at least. Anyway, who the hell would care if the story were published in the *Post*?" Kate never read the *Post* but she had somehow gathered that that was where scandals came home to roost.

Reed put a hand on Kate's arm; with a frown of apology, she subsided lower into the leather couch. "What Kate means, I think," Reed said, "is that we are speaking of something that happened more than half a century ago. Your mother, though perhaps tempted, did not run off with Kate's father. She stayed to serve as an admirable mother to you all. Surely that is what should be remembered."

"That's as may be," William said. "But had it been known that Kate was not the child of our father, she would not have inherited. His will was perfectly clear on this point, as we would expect it to be."

"Are you saying you want me to give you back my share of the inheritance?" Kate asked, without anger. She sounded genuinely curious.

"As I'm sure you are all, as lawyers, aware," Reed remarked, "a child who might possibly be the child of the woman's husband—even if, as in one notorious case, he has been absent for eleven months—such a child is considered to be the husband's, legally and in every other way. Unless your father had explicitly disinherited her in his will—and we know that he did not even suspect that she was not his daughter—she has every right to her inheritance. That was before DNA, of course," he added apologetically.

"We don't want her money," Laurence all but shouted. "William was just pointing out that this is not just an insignificant matter." The other two nodded in agreement.

Kate pulled herself together; she sat up straight, and looked at each of her brothers in turn.

"I'm truly sorry this has happened," she said, speaking slowly, "and had I had a choice, had I been offered the opportunity, I would have prevented it. As you know, Jay came to Laurence first, not to me. Had I been the first to hear of this, I would have . . . " She paused. "To be honest, I don't know what I would have done, but I believe I would not have gone forward without considering your feelings. I never had the opportunity to consider your feelings or my own. Let me also add that Laurence thought of Edith Wharton when he first heard from Jay, and there cannot be, or ever have been, anyone more proper than Edith Wharton's family. Edith Wharton herself, by the way, had a passionate love affair while married, though with more cause than our mother had."

"What on earth do you mean?" David asked.

Kate chose to interpret his question as relating to Edith Wharton. "Edith Wharton," she explained, "had a feckless, unreliable, generally disgraceful husband. Our mother did not. All the same, I just want to point out that this sort of thing can happen in the best of families. The very best."

She sat back, looking apologetic.

"Why the hell are we discussing Edith Wharton?" William shouted.

"The point we want to make here," Laurence said, ignoring William and looking at Reed, "is our desire, certainly justified, to know more about this man, this person. He says he's an architect, but is he? I know his motives may not be sinister, but I, we, would all feel better knowing more about him. Don't you agree, Reed?"

"Of course we both agree," Reed said, taking Kate's hand, whether in sympathy or to shut her up she was not sure. "Did you want me to undertake an investigation? I would of course report all findings to you."

"No need for that," Laurence said, rising. "I just

wanted to be sure we saw eye to eye on the matter, at least to that extent." The other two rose also. Reed and Kate took rather longer to extricate themselves from the deep leather couch. When they were all on their feet, a slightly more amiable atmosphere could be felt.

"We didn't intend to blame you, Kate," William said. "Of course you know that."

"Of course," Kate agreed. She believed that in recent years, certainly since her brothers had all become responsible adults, married and with families, more and more established, richer and richer, they had resented her for a good deal, not least for keeping her name, Fansler, instead of taking Reed's name when, far later than they considered appropriate, she had married him. Kate's carryings-on under the name of Fansler had caused them all embarrassment, and, in addition to rebuking her, they would, if they could, have gladly banished her to the Outer Hebrides. And if they had always blamed her in a general way, they now knew how right they had been: even the circumstances of her birth had turned out to be a disaster.

"We must do our best to shut this man up," David said, and Reed feared the whole discussion might begin all over again. The Fansler men could not believe that Jay did not have a menacing motive. Reed took a firmer grip on Kate's hand and pulled her from the room. Kate waved goodbye as they went.

Reed and Kate began walking uptown, each of them pondering what to make of the Fansler brothers' fears and comments. Kate held Reed's arm, wanting to feel close to him, partly as comfort after the unsettling feelings her brothers always evoked in her, partly because his wonderful good sense compared to them filled her with gratitude. Reed carried her briefcase in his other hand. She knew he was going to speak about the meeting they had just left, and waited for his words.

"They're certain to hire an investigator," Reed said. "No doubt of that. They all but said so."

"Did they? I always hear threats, but nothing definitive about the form the threats will take, if any. I understand the fury in their words, but not the words, as Desdemona more or less put it."

"Desdemona denied her father, and you found yours. Well, I can hardly blame your brothers," Reed said. "I wanted to investigate the man myself. I think it's a way we feel we can get some control in a situation that was so unexpected and startling. Probably it's rational to be suspicious, at least to some degree. What strikes me as intriguing is that you seem the least curious about him, when you might be the most curious."

"I know. I seem more to worry about what difference knowing he's my father makes than about what he's been doing between my birth and now. Which doesn't make much sense, since what he's been doing would tell me what sort of person he is."

"Your brothers," Reed said, squeezing her arm against his body in acknowledgment of her words, "can call upon a lot of influence. I suspect that the investigator they hire may be very well connected indeed."

"Not a poor, foolish amateur like me. What difference does it make if he's well connected?"

"For one thing, he'll have access to criminal and other records."

"Reed. Do you think Jay is, or has been, a common criminal?"

"I don't know. I'm wondering if we should warn him."

"You mean warn him about my brothers but not about your delvings into his past."

Reed laughed. "Mine were superficial and delicate delvings."

Kate stopped walking for a moment and withdrew her arm. "Let's go to a museum," she said. "Let's look at a few wonderful paintings and forget all this nastiness."

"Good idea. The Metropolitan?"

"No. Too big, too spread out, too pullulating."

"Kate! What a word. Surely they don't pullulate at the Met."

"It just means teeming," she said. "Crowded. Like the mackerel-crowded sea."

"What?"

"Yeats. Not to worry. Let's go to the Frick. It's my favorite museum, bespeaking as it does an earlier time when elegance was possible due to the lack of taxes, the lack of regulation, and the exploitation of the working classes."

"In fact," Reed said, "I think Frick did Carnegie's dirty work. But I'm happy to enjoy the art and magnificent decor he has left behind."

" 'The evil men do lives after them; the good is oft interred with their bones.' It seems to have been the other way around with Frick; his lovely museum is certainly good." She put her arm back in his and they walked on.

"Are there any pictures you particularly want to see?" Reed asked.

"Yes," she rather surprised him by saying. "I used to go there with my mother. There are two Holbein portraits that might be titled good and evil: Thomas More and Thomas Cromwell. It's amazing to see how Holbein accomplished it. Then there are the Rembrandts. Actually, the self-portrait at the Met is magnificent and two years later than the one at the Frick, but one has to climb stairs and wander about to find it. And then there is *The Polish Rider*."

"Really, Kate, you amaze me. Here we have been married all these years, and you never mentioned the Frick before, let alone suggested going there."

"It just seemed the right antidote to my Fansler brothers," Kate said. "But you mustn't mind if we just look at those four pictures. We can sweep through the rooms if you want to admire the furnishings, but might you agree not to loiter? I believe in being very object-oriented in museums."

"It's so long since I've been there, I'm happy to follow you in every way," Reed said.

And indeed the luxuriant and tasteful decorations did much to counter the ambience of the Fansler office. Kate and Reed contemplated Kate's four pictures; Reed agreed on the amazing subtlety by which Holbein had made clear his opinion of the two men without failing to produce an acceptable portrait of each. The self-portrait of Rembrandt struck Reed most forcibly.

"Have you ever noticed," he asked, "how few pictures there are of old people, and how most of them seem contrived to deny signs of aging? Rembrandt is different."

Kate looked at the picture for a long time. "Jay is old," she said, "though I never think of him that way. He's older than Rembrandt was when he painted this picture. I know, people live longer now, and in better health. Still, Jay is going along in his seventies. As Falstaff more or less said of someone else, he cannot help but be in his seventies."

"True," Reed said. "I hadn't really thought of his age. No doubt you'll be just as upright and sprightly in your time. Genes you know."

"I shall never be sprightly," Kate said, turning to go. But it did occur to her that her Fansler father had died younger than Jay would; Jay was flourishing.

Nine

FOR SOME DAYS, nothing happened. Kate mentioned to Reed how odd it was that they should be devoting so much time to wondering about a man they had never heard of until some weeks ago; she hadn't kept track, but it wasn't that many weeks, was it? Now when they weren't dreading whatever steps Laurence was taking, or hiring someone to take, they were hoping nothing violent had happened to Jay. Whatever kind of fugitive or adventurer he turned out to be, one hardly, as Reed pointed out to a puzzled Kate, wanted him snuffed out so soon after his dramatic appearance.

"Snuffed out?" Kate asked.

"Well, forced to disappear. Snuffed out of our presence. It's very odd indeed; very odd." So they kept repeating to one another, finding some consolation in this, particularly because, by some silent, never formulated pact, they had not mentioned him to anyone else. (Kate's conversation with Leslie hardly counted; she was not "anyone else.") Reed had no friends toward whom such intimacy was expected. Thus like Laurence, but for different reasons—so they hoped—they kept silent, and could only repeat the same apprehensions over and over to one another, at the same time debating why they should feel so apprehensive about a man they scarcely knew.

And then Laurence was heard from. Abiding by the habits of the established male world he still viewed as basically unchanged, he called Reed, man to man, at Reed's office.

"Well," Laurence barked over the telephone, "I was right. The man's a criminal."

"Oh, yes?" Reed said, waiting for the rest of it.

"He's been in the Witness Protection Program. He left it, and no doubt has now been forced to disappear in fear for his life. Men who leave the Witness Protection Program are murdered more often than not."

"Perhaps," Reed said. "But not everyone in the program is a criminal. Sometimes they are only in danger from others who are criminals."

"Usually they've been criminals themselves who have testified against their associates in return for no sentence and the Witness Protection Program. Everyone knows that."

"Then everyone knows wrong," Reed said, allowing some asperity to creep into his voice. "Terrified witnesses, who may not themselves have committed any crime, are persuaded to testify and promised the Witness Protection Program. I think we ought not to leap to conclusions without more evidence."

"If we get more evidence in time, that's all very well. Meanwhile, I think we better take certain precautions against this man."

"Laurence," Reed said with more patience than he felt, "you yourself mentioned him to Kate and arranged for Kate to meet him. What has brought about this sudden suspicion and accusations?"

"I know, I know. The fact is, I didn't think the man would test out. I didn't for a moment suppose he was Kate's father. I thought she'd hand over her blood sample and then we'd go after the impostor. And it happened my wife or maybe my daughter was discussing Edith Wharton, and the whole comparison seemed amusing at the time. If you intend to tell me I should have known better, I won't be able to deny it."

"Meaning," Reed said, "you thought you would get a chance to make fun of Kate and show her up."

"I can hardly stop you from saying what you want in her defense," Laurence said coldly. "After all, she is your wife. But she certainly doesn't show much respect for her origins."

"Kate needs no defense, mine or anyone else's. You behaved like a cad, and now you want to hunt down her father—and he is her father—to make up for your silly indiscretion. It's hardly a worthy motive, Laurence."

"Since you have no wish to protect my sister, and since she is too much of a fool to defend herself against a criminal, I feel my actions are quite justified. Good afternoon." And Laurence hung up. Reed told himself that he had not handled that conversation very well, and that he would have to do something to make sure that Laurence continued to tell him the results of his, Laurence's, investigation.

He said as much to Kate that evening.

"Your father was in the Witness Protection Program; that's what Laurence's sleuth uncovered," he announced to her in conclusion.

"What?"

"The Witness Protection Program."

"You mean there really is such a thing? I thought it was just something they'd made up for TV cop shows."

"Really, Kate. It's not a good idea to lose one's grip on reality. There is such a program, and then there are TV shows."

"Don't be so sure, Reed. We live in a postmodern age, which freely translated means it is no longer possible, let alone easy, to tell the difference between reality and simulated reality."

"I see. Like that *Wag the Dog* movie, where they managed to convince everyone there was a war on when it was only a simulated war."

"That's the idea. Could you tell photographs of a tornado from a tornado created on a computer? No, you couldn't. I believe in the dinosaurs in movies, but I don't think they're part of a government program or of reality. When it comes to anything more recent than dinosaurs, I'm far from sure."

"If we can postpone this discussion of postmodernism, frightening as it is, let me assure you that there is indeed a Witness Protection Program, and I'm willing to believe Jay was in it. What we have to discover is why."

"I only hope if Laurence finds out, he'll tell us."

"I was quite rude to him today; he is a maddening person. But I shall have to throw myself on his mercy in the hope that he'll keep me informed."

"If I know Laurence," Kate said, "his desire to gloat and to prove his clout means he'll tell you. But it never hurts to get on his good side with flattery and bullshit if you want something from him. I haven't wanted anything in years, but recollections of childhood dramas can be summoned up."

Reed did phone and apologize to Laurence for his unfortunate remarks, to which Laurence, with a stab at affability, responded that he did not blame Reed for being troubled by this dreadful situation. Reed managed to end the call without responding with the irritation he felt.

The next day Kate telephoned Reed's office. This was unusual in itself; he could not remember the last time she had called him at his office; any plans for the day were usually confirmed before they parted in the morning.

"Clara has called in some alarm, and so has the superintendent," Kate said on the phone. "Two men, well dressed, turned up saying they had orders or a warrant or anyway the right to search our apartment. Clara, whom we now salute as a prize among cleaning women, not that we didn't know it before, refused to let them in. I like to think that Banny standing beside Clara also had its effect. They had come upstairs with the doorman, who didn't want to let them in either, but agreed to take them this far. The men apparently were quite good with their demands, but our defenders held firm. Then started the questions: had there been an older man around—they described Jay, or I think they were describing Jay. They quizzed Clara and the doorman, and the other man in the lobby, and finally the doorman called the superintendent, who asked them to leave. What strikes me as sinister here, Reed, is that these men had enough presence and authority to avoid a quick refusal. Do you think one of us should go home?"

"I take it they are gone."

"So the superintendent said, and I thanked him and kept insisting that such people should never be let in under any circumstances. If they come when we are home, then we will go down to the lobby to meet them. Does that sound about right?"

"Of course. The question is, who were they and what did they want?"

"I assume they wanted Jay."

"Very likely, but not certain. They may have been studying the layout, so to speak. Casing the joint."

"Whatever for? Anyway, they kept asking the doorman, the superintendent, Clara, even Banny for all I know, if there had been any sign of a man around our apartment, visiting us, staying with us, anything. They were all able to assure him that there was no such person. I got the impression the men were convinced by these sturdy denials."

"I don't know why they might have been getting an idea of the layout, in addition to finding out if Jay were with us or had been with us; that's what I want to know, or at least to figure out. I'll be done here in a while, and I'll head home and talk to the men before their shift ends, just to satisfy myself about what questions were asked."

"Good," Kate said. "I'll see you there then. Ought I to worry? I will worry in any case, but have I grounds for serious worry or only generalized anxiety?"

"Somewhere in between, I think. When will you be home?"

"I'll try to make it by five. No doubt I shall listen with less than my usual patience and sympathy to whoever comes in my office hour."

"Unlikely. The question is, really, why do these unofficial men want Jay, and how did they know to look for him at our house?"

"So many questions; so few answers." Kate sighed and hung up.

"What I suspect," Reed said later, when they were sitting with their drinks, "is that these chaps who didn't get in here know that Jay has left the Witness Protection Program and want him now, before he can tell the authorities anything. Which leaves even more questions: what did he do? Why was he in the Witness Protection Program? Why did he leave it? What is it he could tell that would endanger our visitors and has them so frightened?"

"Reed, I know it sounds naive, foolish, and unbefitting my professional station in life, but what the hell *is* the Witness Protection Program? I do gather, I really do, that it consists of hiding people who have given information to the police or the FBI or someone for which they could be killed. But how often does that happen outside of television cop shows?"

"Since you had already uttered this same disbelief concerning the Witness Protection Program, I made use today of LexisNexis and found that someone had written about the program for the *New York Times Magazine*.[*] Here, I'll leave it for you to read on your own. Just to note that the wife of the man being moved into the Witness Protection Program as described in this article agrees with your disbelief. When she realizes that she must abandon her life for another one utterly different, she says: 'I couldn't believe it was real. All that time I didn't think that this type of organization really existed. I thought it was just in the movies.' It was real enough. She and her husband, together with their three children, would begin a new life in a new place where they knew no one, would have different names, and be permitted to take virtually nothing of their past with them into their new existence. The woman who had thought this organization existed only in the movies would never see her parents and her siblings again."

"Could they leave the program?"

"Yes. But at least by 1996 when this article was published, no one in the program had been murdered, but thirty who had left the program had been murdered."

"So the odds are that Jay will be murdered."

"The odds are that he is in danger; serious danger."

Kate shook her head. "I can't believe this is happening; the normal reaction under the circumstances, no doubt. One has to accept that Jay was either a criminal testifying against another criminal,

[*]Robert Sabbag, "The Invisible Family," 11 February 1996.

or that at the least, he was involved with criminals, testified against them, and was thus in danger for his life and went into the Witness Protection Program. Does that seem a fair statement of the facts?"

"It does to me," Reed said. "But we are talking about a program, or organization, which is hardly open about its operations or any facts about those taken into it. I don't think it's quite time to conclude that your father was a criminal; the most we can assume is that he was a witness, and that that puts him in danger."

"That still leaves us with our own facts—that he shows up in our lives, establishes himself irrefutably, thanks to modern science, as my father, while leaving us to guess what his motive was."

"For showing up? For leaving the program?"

"All of that. But why is connecting himself to me the advisable action for him to take at this time? How does it serve his, if not criminal, at least hardly legal or conventionally upright purposes?"

"My dear, I hardly know what to say. We can't demand that he appear and explain himself. We certainly can't demand to be told about him by the Witness Protection Program; I doubt even Laurence's influence could accomplish that. I realize it's no use asking you not to brood about it, because of course you can hardly help brooding about it."

"Are you sure Laurence couldn't find out more from the Witness Protection people?" Kate asked. "If there's one thing we all know about the government and Washington bureaus and so forth, it's that money and power—which are probably the same thing—can buy you any information or influence you want. After all, Nixon could get the FBI to go after people who openly opposed the Vietnam War."

"I don't know how far Laurence's arm reaches. I could ask him; you could do your best to persuade him at least to set queries into motion. He has to feel some responsibility to you in all this, quite apart from his own fears and angers. But think, Kate. Do you really want to do that?"

"I don't know what I really want to do. I hate the thought of encouraging Laurence against Jay, if you want to know the truth; at least I think I hate the thought. On the other hand, whatever nefarious practices Laurence had indulged in, they are, so to speak, accepted nefarious practices."

"Kate, I'm not sure . . ."

"Remember when George W. Bush was elected president, or anyway, when he achieved the presidency? He had taken a lot of campaign money from the oil and the mining industries, and the first thing he did upon taking office was to reject his campaign promise to lower emissions standards, and to revoke Clinton's attempt to reduce the amount of arsenic in our water. Don't you think Laurence had a part in all that, or something very like it?"

"Do I take that to mean you don't want to encourage Laurence in his pursuit of Jay or that you do? I don't say I am entirely in accord with your judgments of Laurence; you are rather being carried away, if you'll forgive my mentioning it. On the other hand, I do concur in your taking no action, at least for now, if that's what you've decided. As you know, I'll back you in whatever you decide to do, as long as it is not criminal. I've no desire to be swept off with you into the Witness Protection Program; our life here is certainly worth preserving, as I hope you agree."

"Well," Kate said, getting up to head for the kitchen and decisions about dinner, "at least I, unlike the woman in your article, would not mind being forced never to see any of my family again. On the other hand, I don't think I'd care to settle down somewhere in the South or the Midwest. I'm a Northeasterner at heart; and after all, would any southerner or midwesterner want to be plunked down in New York to start life all over again? Of course not."

"A bit dramatically put, but I'm glad of the conclusion."

"I don't condone Jay's actions whatever they were; if they landed him in the Witness Protection Program, they are no doubt beyond approbation. But I do feel I owe him something for demonstrating that I am not, and have never been, a Fansler. I don't know how I feel about this discovery of my paternal heritage, but I do know I can at last understand why nothing my family stood for seemed to me desirable. I'm also proud to learn that I went a different way than either becoming the anarchical member of a family who is forced to the enactment of violent insurrection, or someone like Edith Wharton who turns to writing but never abandons the manners of her culture, however much it made her suffer. Me, I just didn't belong, I knew it, and now I know why."

"As I keep saying, you might have turned out very much the same as a real Fansler."

"No, Reed, I've decided. Jay made the difference.

I can't think why, if he had never appeared, I wouldn't have realized that. I guess it's because the question never came up; because I never really thought about it."

Ten

DURING THE NEXT week nothing whatever happened. Reed and Kate promised each other to resist any temptation to do anything about Jay. As they recognized, the temptation was great to make something happen: perhaps to call Laurence, urging him on; perhaps to try to probe further into Jay's life. They yearned to set some action, any action, into motion, but bound by their mutual agreement, they abstained. By well into the following week, as a result of this forbearance, they found it increasingly easier to let hours pass without thinking of Kate's father and his putative criminal career. Kate even stopped obsessing about what such a father meant to her sense of herself. They had even begun to wonder if they might not stagger through the rest of their lives without ever encountering Jay again.

And then, as suddenly as he had disappeared, he reappeared. One morning, when Kate was home alone with Banny, the back doorbell rang. Supposing it to be a delivery or Con Edison to read a meter, Kate opened the door to confront a painter. The back-elevator man explained that this man was working with the company painting the lobby and some of the halls, and he wanted to come in to examine the front hall outside of Kate's apartment. The painter was slumped against the elevator wall, his body language indicating annoyance at having to examine the hall, at permission having to be asked. Upon Kate's nodding agreement with this plan, the painter slouched into the apartment.

"Shall I wait?" the elevator man asked.

"Don't bother," the painter said. "I'll walk down. I have to get some measurements." And with that, the elevator closed.

"This way," Kate said.

"It's me," the painter said. And the slouching painter took off his cap, straightened up, his whole demeanor changed, and Kate recognized Jay.

"It's an old trick," he said, "but still a good one. You kind of join up with some outfit that's doing some work in the house, and try to get past the staff; this fellow is so lazy he couldn't bother to check me out. And why should he? I'm with the outfit that's doing the painting. They send different painters around each day—the boss comes to check them and their work out at the end of the afternoon. As long as I avoid him, I'm okay. It has to be supposed that he knows what painters he's hired, but the painters don't always know each other."

Kate stared at him. So many questions crowded into her mind that she was beyond expressing any of them; her astonishment was palpable.

"It's all right," Jay said. "Have you a room you don't use much; one with the shades drawn, or able to be drawn?"

Kate took a moment to register the question. "Well," she said, "there's a maid's room. We don't use it, except as a sort of attic. In here." The "maid's room" opened out of the kitchen. It contained a cot, a bureau, some shelves bulging with unassorted items, and a number of boxes from computers, printers, and VCRs stacked around. There was not much room to move.

"We could throw out most of this," Kate said. "We also have a bin in the basement where we could put what we want to keep. We just never get around to it. If we got rid of some of these boxes . . ."

"Don't get rid of anything," he said. "Don't do anything unusual. This is fine." He pulled the drawn shade aside to ascertain that the room looked out on the courtyard, ten stories down. The room across the way also had its shades down.

"There's a lamp somewhere," Kate said.

"No lamp. No light must show. The thing is, Kate, I'd like to hang out here for a day or two. They've already determined I'm not here, which makes it a good place to lie low."

"Won't the back-elevator man wonder why you didn't leave?"

"No. He'll assume I walked down as I said I would. Anyway, he's a lazy fellow. If we can manage not to arouse his curiosity, he won't bother about me. Is it all right if I stay then?"

Kate pulled herself together. She thought of calling Reed, and then remembered that he was in court and would not be available.

"Have you something, anything, to eat?" he asked. "And some water? I'll stay in here. It's even got a bathroom; better than I could have hoped."

"Are you saying you can't come into the kitchen?"

"Better not. I don't want anyone to catch even a glimpse of me through a window. A piece of bread would do."

"I'll make you a sandwich. Anything to drink besides water?"

"Coffee would be welcome, but I don't want to bother . . ."

"You want to hide out in our apartment, which is probably some sort of federal crime, but you don't want me to bother making a cup of coffee. Well, I'll make the sandwich and the coffee; I'll bring them to you in here. But there is a price: I want some sort of explanation; I want to know what the hell is going on with you."

"It's a bargain," Jay said. "But please, Kate. I haven't committed a criminal offense; I'm not a criminal under any law. I wouldn't have burdened you in this way, except that someone is trying to kill me. I may decide to let him kill me, but I thought, well, if I hide out with Kate, at least I can explain all this. I gather Reed has been doing some detecting, having spotted the lacunae in my résumé. And I thought it was such a clever résumé."

Kate went to make the sandwich and to put up the coffee. She felt that she could use a cup herself. Banny, who always monitored the doors, back and front, when anyone rang, sat looking at Jay calmly, but steadily. The slightest of rumbles had risen in her throat when he entered the apartment; these had now subsided.

103

Kate brought a tray with the sandwich, the coffee-pot, two cups, and a glass of water into the maid's room. It was an extremely odd place to be holding a conversation, but Kate had every intention of holding it. Jay had spotted a folding chair behind some boxes and opened it. "Chair or cot?" he asked Kate.

"Chair," Kate said. She put the tray on the cot next to Jay, and poured the coffee. He drank the whole glass of water without pausing, and then began eating the sandwich; his hunger was evident. Kate sipped her coffee. They sat with their knees touching as, Kate thought, in some old-time spy movie. She picked up one of the large cartons and heaved it on top of another, which allowed her to move her chair back an inch or so.

Dramatic sentences began to drift into Kate's mind, such as: he gave me life and now he might kill me; can anything be said for having a criminal as a father? how much is owed a father, particularly one you haven't seen for fifty or so years? She uttered none of them, banishing them from her thoughts. "Start at the beginning," she said.

"What is the beginning?"

"When you left my mother."

"I could start there. But I think what you want to know now is why I was in the Witness Protection Program, why I left it, and why I'm in danger now. That's not quite the story of my life, but it's a good bit of it."

"All right," Kate said. "Tell me that story."

"After I left your mother, for the next twenty years, life was just as the résumé reported it, with one significant exception, to which I'll come eventually. Let's skip over that for now. I went to architecture school, just as the résumé said. I worked on odd construction jobs. I started an architecture firm with a partner, the man who is still my partner, though he knows nothing of all this. He knows I took a leave but not what for or anything about it. We worked on the restoration of historic buildings. As you know, we started in New York but soon moved west, to my great relief. Not only because I was farther from your mother, but because restoration work in New York City can get really nasty."

"How's that?" Kate asked. Nothing, Reed would have said had he been there, could keep Kate from asking for information, even under the most extraordinary circumstances.

Jay did not seem to find the question strange. "Well, say there's an historic building that needs to be rebuilt; it's in a stage beyond disrepair, definitely in need of attention. The owner, constricted on every side by the Landmark Commission—a very good organization, by the way, organized when the great old Penn Station was torn down without a thought in the 1960s, I think—where was I? The owner asks and gets permission to add a few stories to his old building, on which he is spending a fortune. Now come the folks in brownstones next door who fear a shadow will be cast on them by the extra stories. In fact a shadow will be cast. So the poor architect is bombarded on all sides, by the owner, by the neighbors, by the Landmark Commission. It's not so bad in other cities."

"I see. Do go on."

"There we were, established in the West, a firm

with an excellent reputation, and undertaking interesting work in restoration when, sometime in the Seventies, I cut loose."

"You left the firm?"

"Call it, as I did, a leave of absence. I wanted some time to look around and think; as a partner, I continued to get some income from the firm."

"Were you married by then?"

"No. That came later. The problem was, I had been involved in a crime, well, a kind of crime. I can't explain the reasons to you now, and I'm not sure I could have done a very coherent job of explaining them then. I became the accomplice of an art thief."

Kate stood up from the folding chair, which was already making her feel cramped. Jay started to get up also, but she pushed him back onto the cot. "Is this some nonsense I'm supposed to listen to with innocent belief? Are you making all this up as you go along?"

"Am I indeed? A rational question. I thought I knew why at the time, but in retrospect it's as unbelievable to me as it obviously is to you. It's connected to Shakespeare in a way. I think I better stand up, too. No, I won't stand up with you; I think I might stretch out on the cot. Would that offend you? I haven't had much sleep lately."

"Go right ahead," Kate said. "The cot may not be long enough, and it's certainly not very comfortable. We used to keep it for use when nieces and nephews unexpectedly turned up to spend a day or two."

Jay stretched out on it, his head lying flat, his feet dangling over the bottom of the cot. Kate waited with what she considered commendable patience, then turned to ignite him with another question.

He was asleep. She looked at him. His was a sleep of extreme exhaustion; it might continue for hours. She thought of covering him with something, and then decided that she would not offer a single further indulgence. She had probably gone too far already in letting him fall asleep in their maid's room. She closed the door of the room and left him to it.

When Reed came home she went to greet him in the hall. It occurred to her that since the advent of Jay, she and Reed had taken to waiting for each other in the hall, a clear sign that the even tenor of their lives had been disrupted.

"What now?" he said, before she spoke.

"He's here."

"Who?"

"Jay."

"What do you mean, *here*?"

"Here, in the apartment. Actually, in the maid's room, which he is determined not to leave even for a moment. He's fallen asleep."

"Kate, are you out of your mind?"

"Don't start huffing and puffing until I tell you what happened. I was more or less trapped. Well, I could have dialed 911, but failing that, I had no other recourse."

Reed sat down on one of the chairs in the hall and seemed to lose himself in unhappy contemplations.

"What on earth are we going to do?" he asked.

"Well, I rather thought we would hear him out. He started telling me about getting into a life of crime—art theft, apparently—but simply sank into sleep the minute he stretched out on the cot. He's very tired."

"*He's* very tired. Kate, you do realize that harboring a criminal is a felony, among other things. I know he's your father, but do you want to go to jail for him, or worse, have to testify against him?"

"Why don't we sit down in the living room and talk about this calmly?"

"Calmly! You've never advised calm in your life. You're always the one I have to pacify. I hate what this whole damn business is doing to us."

"Let's talk about it. If you insist on calling the police or the FBI or the Witness Protection Program or whomever, I'll go along with it. But let's chew it over first. How about a drink?"

"I hope you didn't offer Jay a drink."

"He doesn't drink, remember? Oh, no, you weren't there. The first time I met him—which feels like a century ago—he said he didn't drink. His mother was an alcoholic, he said. He asked for coffee. Not then, I don't mean, just now. Then he asked for tea."

"I don't believe his mother was an alcoholic. I don't believe he had a mother. Were it not for DNA, I wouldn't believe he had the smallest connection with you. Did you know that men now can get on the Web and send in their specimens and that of their children to find out if the children are really theirs?"

"Reed, please sit down. We will settle what to do about Jay one way or the other in a few hours, when he wakes up, or when we wake him. Meanwhile, I can't help feeling a drink might lessen the tension, temporarily at least."

To her relief, Reed smiled. Kate didn't doubt that it was his knowledge of the law, particularly criminal law, that was troubling him so profoundly. But for the moment for her, she had to admit to herself, curiosity was winning out over fear. For the moment.

Thou art thy mother's glass
and she in thee
Calls back the lovely April of
her prime.

Eleven

THEY LOOKED IN on Jay from time to time, but he slept, as the old saying goes, like the dead. Kate and Reed ate dinner, but hardly felt able to return to their studies at the other end of the apartment from the maid's room. Theirs was an old apartment, built in the days when everyone who could afford to live there had at least one sleep-in maid; thus these apartments built in the twenties or earlier each had a maid's room. It was small, with an attached small bathroom, and in the years since World War II no one but Fanslers and their ilk had household help who hung around for more than a few hours, let alone overnight. A maid's room now served other purposes.

Occasionally, a child occupied it, but that was rare. Usually, as with Kate and Reed, it served as an "attic." Some who had redone their kitchens had broken down walls and included the maid's room in their enlarged, modern, magazine-worthy cooking environment. Then there were those in large, rent-stabilized apartments, clinging to the low rent, who secretly, and illegally, housed lodgers in their maid's room to expand their shrinking income. Whether any other maid's room had ever harbored a man running for his life Kate doubted. Meanwhile, she and Reed found it impossible to get down to work, and so they hovered—in the living room, the kitchen, the hall. Kate took Banny out for a walk; they returned to find that Jay was still asleep. Reed was still hovering.

"We can't spend the night like this," Reed said. "I think we had better wake him."

"We could sleep in shifts," Kate said.

"The fact is, we could ignore him. He's not likely to leave the room; we can just let him sit there. After all there is a bathroom and running water."

"But would we sleep very well?" Kate asked.

"The hell with it," Reed said. "Let's wake him."

They knocked on the closed door of the maid's room, not wanting to walk in on him unannounced, though it occurred to them both that such courtesy seemed slightly comical under the circumstances. But there was no answer to their knock. Reed opened the door and peered in.

"He's still sound asleep; I'm going to wake him."

"Then what?" Kate asked.

"Then he can start talking."

Reed had to shake Jay, who woke suddenly and leapt up in fear. Then the knowledge of where he was returned to him. "Sorry about that," he said to Reed. "I haven't had so extended a sleep in, well, quite a while. I must have felt safe, because I was certainly out cold."

"Why don't you wash up?" Reed said. "And then Kate and I would like to talk to you. Are you willing to try the kitchen if we lower the blind?"

"Do you usually lower it?"

"No, we don't usually lower it."

"Then let's sit in here, if you can put up with it."

"Are you really suggesting, or fearing, that whoever is after you is so intent and so observant that even the lowering of a shade that is usually up would signal something?"

"I can't tell how much he's able to watch, of course," Jay said. "But he's capable of anything. Killing me is his only aim in life; he has no other. It has become his obsession. He may decide I must be here because I'm not anywhere else, but I think this is safe enough for now if there's no indication of my presence."

Reed, leaving Jay to use the bathroom facilities, reported this conversation to Kate, who was making coffee. When Jay beckoned to them from the small room that, for now at least, was his, or so it seemed, Reed and Kate entered, Kate carrying yet another tray with a coffeepot, cups, and a plate of ginger cookies.

Jay took it from her and placed it, sideways, in the center of the cot. "Why don't you sit at one end?" he said to Reed. "I'll sit at the other, with our legs out as far as they can go, and Kate can sit in the chair and put her legs on the cot between us when we remove the tray. Does that suit you?"

And so they settled themselves. Kate at first was content to sit in the chair with her feet crossed, drinking her coffee, but after a while she was glad of the chance, when Jay had moved the tray onto a box, to stretch her legs across the center of the cot.

"We are all three too tall for this caper," she said. Reed and Jay were both tall men, and Kate was tall for a woman, or at least for a woman of her generation. They grew women bigger now, she had noticed, which was, in her opinion, a good thing. One might not play basketball, but it must be pleasant to know that one could.

"I don't know what we're going to do about you," Reed said to Jay, "but while we're all hiding out here like burglars caught on the premises, why don't you begin the story of how you got here?"

"Do you want an outline or details?" Jay asked.

"Outline first, details later, if required," Reed said.

"I take it you both know about the Witness Protection Program."

"Not a great deal. Just what we read in the magazines and newspapers," Reed said. Kate suspected he knew a bit more than that, but nodded to affirm his statement.

"Then I won't start there. I'll start with a crime I committed, or helped to commit, in the late 1950s or thereabouts. It was art theft. We broke into a small museum and stole a painting."

"We?" Kate asked.

"There were three of us. My friend, whose plan it was, me, and the man who is now trying to kill me."

Jay seemed to be waiting for a response, and was rather at a loss when none came. And what response could he have expected us to give, Kate asked herself. She found this whole situation so bizarre that almost nothing Jay might say could make it more

113

so. This man, her father, into his seventies, a man her husband considered capable of many and assorted criminalities, huddled with his newfound daughter and her husband in a small, back room, speaking of how he had committed a theft.

"Go on," Reed said.

"Let me diverge from the outline for a moment. I loved your mother"—he faced Kate—"as one is supposed to love only in romances and old-style movies. Remember that you mentioned *Brief Encounter* to me that day by the pond?"

"I remember. That film must have been made very long ago; it's not even in color."

"Around the time you were born, I think, or a year or two earlier. I also saw it revived. You remember the story?"

"They meet in a railroad station, fall in love, and then part in the railroad station."

"They fall in love forever; at least, he does. When they must part because they're both married, he says to her: 'I will love you all my life,' or words to that effect."

"So you mentioned when we sat by the pond. And there's a good chance he will love her all his life, since they will never meet again," Kate said.

"What a cynic you are."

"I'm not the least cynical. But perhaps we had better postpone this discussion." Reed looked as though he might explode if this sideline on love was not short-circuited.

"Most people doubt that kind of love," Jay said. "Anyway, just accept for the moment that leaving your mother changed my life, changed how I looked at things, how I judged them."

114

"So stealing art was justified because you had lost your love," Reed said. His tone was harsh.

"Not stealing any art. I don't think I would have considered any other crime, certainly not another art theft. But I had this friend, and he had lost his love, too."

"Under similar circumstances, arousing your sympathy?" Reed asked.

"Not similar, no. His passion was for a painting." He paused, as though expecting an interruption, but none came.

"It was a painting both he and his mother had loved; it had hung in their living room, where she could see it from the chair she always sat in. He remembered, as a very small child, sitting with her while she told him the story of the painting. Inspired by Shakespeare's *The Tempest*, it portrayed Prospero revealing to Miranda the story of how they had come to be shipwrecked on that island. The painter, my friend said, had caught the relationship between father and daughter in a way that seemed to him, when he was a child, to picture the bond between his mother and him. Anyway, his parents divorced, his father walked out, blaming his mother for the destruction of him and, he said, his son, and he had taken the picture and sold it, either out of revenge or for what money it could bring. When my friend was grown, and his mother had become ill, he hired someone to find the picture for him, if possible. His mother said it had been painted in the nineteenth century by someone well known, if not exactly famous, which seemed to suggest it might turn up somewhere. In fact, it turned

115

up in a small—well, hardly large—museum in San Francisco."

"And your friend persuaded you to help him steal it," Reed finished for him.

"Yes, that's it, more or less. That's the outline. There are more details."

"Let's hear a few of the details of the theft. I take it you succeeded."

"Yes, we did. The third man—the one who now wants to kill me—thought we might as well take a few more pictures while we were at it, but my friend and I dissuaded him. We got away with my friend's mother's picture. He was able to return it to her, to her great delight."

"I assume he didn't tell her the details of where and how he had retrieved it."

"I think he just said he had found it by a lucky accident. She didn't press him for details; she simply cried for happiness. When she died some years later, my friend mailed it back to the museum we had stolen it from; anonymously, of course."

"His mother was, I fear, a more trusting soul than we," Reed said. "But we did not know your friend. Might we, unlike her, press for a few more details?" Kate listened to this exchange with a feeling of suspension, able neither to believe or disbelieve, to doubt or to refuse to doubt. She left it to Reed to move the story along as he saw fit, planning to return for more specificity here or there if she should want it.

"How did you bring it off? The theft of the picture, I mean. Are museums always so lacking in proper security?"

"In fact, as I learned then and since, most of them

116

are. The most famous art theft in America is that of the Isabella Stewart Gardner Museum in Boston."

"I remember," Kate said. "They stole paintings by Rembrandt and Vermeer and others."

"I followed that robbery with great interest, as you might imagine, having been in the racket myself," Jay said, with what was probably meant as irony. "The lack of security was astonishing, but not atypical by any means. The guards were low-paid, and too easily persuaded to let in the crooks, posing as policemen. None of the art stolen had an alarm attached that would have sounded when the paintings, or whatever, were removed. The stolen art was not insured, which meant that there was no insurance company to undertake the retrieval or offer large rewards. And so on. That was in 1990, and the stolen paintings and other objects have never been recovered. The attempts to find the art have all ended in frustration."

"But what can anybody do with art that famous once he's got it?" Kate asked. "It can't be sold, it can't be exhibited. Is there always some eccentric millionaire who paid for the theft and who then keeps the stolen painting, or whatever it is, in a secret room where he gloats over it alone and unobserved?"

"Thefts are not necessarily for money," Jay said. "The *Mona Lisa* was stolen from the Louvre in 1911 by a madman who worked as a cleaner in the museum. They did get it back in time, though."

"I look forward, indeed I eagerly look forward, to the day when we can discuss the whole subject of art theft," Reed said. "For the moment, however, before my legs cramp up and we all are afflicted with severe muscle spasms, might we get to the reason why you are hiding out here? We can fill the lacunae in later, if need be. Why, if possible in a sentence, is this man trying to kill you?"

"In a sentence?" Jay asked. "Hard to put in a sentence. Let me see. This man is trying to kill me because I testified against him and sent him to prison. When he got out, which he ought not to have done, he set about looking for me. Decades of rage have left him obsessed and with no other aim in life. I've opted out of the Witness Protection Program; you don't get a second chance at that. So either he will kill me or—what? I won't stay here long. Just long enough to think of something. Believe me, Reed, Kate. When I set about becoming reacquainted with my daughter I didn't know that that man had got out of prison. I would never have approached you had I known. I'm sorrier about all this than I can say—but those must seem empty words to you."

Reed stood up, and Kate stood once he had. "Go back to sleep," Reed said. "We'll look in on you in the morning." He and Kate maneuvered themselves into a position to leave, having folded up the chair and recovered the tray; it was then that they noticed Banny lying next to the doorway to the maid's room.

Kate laughed, Banny's presence having provided relief from the tension. "Well," Kate said, "if Banny didn't even try to get in here with us, you've got to know how crowded it was."

In their bedroom, Kate asked Reed if he felt any less animosity toward Jay after what they had heard.

"Perhaps," Reed said. "The question is whether

or not I believe him. The story is probably true, more or less, but his motives for helping to steal the picture remain a little cloudy."

"He's my father," Kate said, "and I do foolish things. As Hamlet wisely put it for our purposes, 'I am myself indifferent honest; but yet I could accuse me of such things that it were better my mother had not borne me.' You have to admit, that's marvelously apposite."

Reed decided to ignore the reference to Kate's or Hamlet's mother. "Because I believe you, Kate, and know you to be honest, am I to believe him? Lear had dishonest daughters."

"Lear was a fool who chose not to believe the only honest daughter he had."

"I do balk at the idea of you having a criminal for a father, a real criminal, even with the excuse of losing his only love. Still, the father of his friend had no right to take the picture."

"I think you might chance trusting him, at least until he is proved altogether dishonest. 'We are arrant knaves all; believe none of us.' That, on the other hand, was Hamlet's advice."

"And yours."

"And mine," Kate said. "But, obviously, with reservations."

What should I do but tend
Upon the hours and terms of
your desire?
I have no precious time at all
to spend
Nor services to do, till you
require.

Twelve

THE NEXT DAY, Friday, Kate and Reed, spelling each other, were able to be home so that Jay was never alone in the apartment. Neither of them, if asked, could have explained their powerful disinclination to leave Jay in the apartment unattended, but, explicable or not, they acknowledged their apprehensions and were guided by them.

Clara would not come to clean until the following Tuesday. Something, anything, had to be done about Jay before then. It was, indeed, true that Clara did not enter the maid's room; it was impossible to clean, and the agreement that it would be ignored during her weekly visit was well established. Nonetheless, Kate and Reed did not intend to leave her alone in the apartment with a strange man of whose presence she was ignorant.

At the same time, neither of them felt an immediate need to continue their conversation with him, or to listen to his recounting of his life. Kate pointed out to Reed that Desdemona had loved Othello "for the dangers [he] had passed, and he loved her that she did pity them."

"I feel somewhat the same," Kate said, "although he is my father. Do you find that odd, or distressing?"

"No. But I do think it interferes with an altogether objective view of the situation before us," Reed said.

"Meaning?"

"Meaning I need to think, that's all. And having thought, if what I think is even remotely productive, I need to act. It may turn out that I need to hear more of Jay's adventures before I can act. At the moment, I need to put my feet up and cogitate."

"Well," Kate said, after a pause, "I had thought of going to Boston. Perhaps I could fly up early tomorrow, and be back that night, or early the following morning. Would that suit your needs and enhance your cogitations? You would have to take Banny for all her walks."

"Why Boston?"

"It's a long time since I've seen Selma Rodney. And she is an art historian; might not art historians, or at any rate assistant curators, know something about art theft? It's a subject that has taken a remarkable hold on my imagination."

"Surely there are art historians and curators in New York."

"No doubt. But Selma is an old student and an old friend. And somehow by consulting her in Boston I shan't feel that she's likely to want immediately to pursue further inquiries into my sudden new interest in the subject of art thieves."

"Yes, I see. And you want to demonstrate that

you trust me with this situation, at least for twenty-four hours, and you wish to grant me my need to think alone and uninterruptedly."

"Let's just say it's a journey that seems nicely to serve us both. You will remember, however, that Jay needs to eat, at least occasionally. You might want to check on him from time to time in any case; there is always the danger of his succumbing to claustrophobia and despair."

"Kate, you are either a very wise woman, or a frightened one. Perhaps both. I think a day away from here, from him, from me, would be an excellent idea. And who knows—Selma might just drop a useful hint of some sort, as well as providing information about art theft."

And so Kate set off for Boston, having called Selma who declared herself delighted at the chance to spend a day with Kate, and happy to forego any other plans.

Kate took the shuttle to Boston, and found Selma waiting for her at the airport. "I wasn't sure I could make it," Selma said, "and then I found I could. You never change, you know," she added, smiling at Kate and taking her bag.

"Gray hairs," Kate said. "And all the other changes those gray hairs represent. You don't exactly change much yourself," she added.

But sitting in the car beside Selma, and later, settled across from her at Selma's kitchen table, Kate realized that, in truth, she could hardly have described Selma, had she been asked. Why, she wondered, do I never really *look* at people? That's not true, I do look. But I can't seem to remember faces
122

or even whole persons. I do register if someone is six feet six or five feet three, but not much in between; I'd be a total loss trying to describe someone to a police artist. Whenever you meet a character in books, Kate had noticed, he or she is always described from hair to boots. A detective in a mystery may be face-to-face with a suspect, but we are told how the man or woman is dressed and everything else about them before a question is asked. Is Selma wearing a skirt or trousers? Kate suddenly asked herself. She leaned over the table and peered at Selma's legs; she was wearing a long skirt.

"Lost something?" Selma asked.

"I've suddenly realized that while I recognized you instantly, I couldn't have described you to save my life."

"Have you just become aware of that?" Selma asked.

"Do you mean it's obvious?"

"Of course. Your students have always noticed it. Until we spoke, you sometimes couldn't tell us apart if there was even a superficial resemblance."

"How frightful. And I've been thinking myself an observant person. How deluded we all are, or I am."

"But you are observant. You remember every conversation, every paper a student ever wrote, and, we all suspected, every word you ever read. You're just not into seeing, and I'm not sure most people are, except maybe in books," she added, unconsciously echoing Kate's thoughts.

"I mentioned once to Reed," Kate said, "that rooms are always described also in great detail. Do you think I could describe this room?"

123

"Since you've been in it for all of five minutes, I doubt it. Is this really worrying you?"

"No. It just occurred to me. As an art historian and a curator, you must notice people and paintings and the looks of things, surely?"

"Probably more than you do. That's no doubt connected to why I left graduate school in literature for graduate school in art history, with your kind and active encouragement. Is this what you wanted to discuss?"

"No. That was just idle chatter," Kate said. But she was in fact wondering if her failure ever to have taken note of her difference from the other Fanslers was connected to this odd disability, or if she had developed the disability so as not to notice the difference. Certainly none of the other Fanslers had noticed it; perhaps it was a Fansler gene. If I don't watch out, I'm going to take up Freudian analysis, she warned herself.

"What I was hoping," Kate said, "was that you could tell me something about art theft."

Selma stared at Kate for a moment, and then laughed. "Whatever you wanted to ask about, I knew I'd never be able to guess it. On the other hand, I could now describe you from top to toe. Shall I?"

"Please, no. What about art theft?"

"Am I to know the reason for this particular inquiry?" Kate shrugged. "Very well, no questions asked," Selma said. Kate had been a crucial figure in Selma's life, as teacher, as supporter, ultimately as friend. "The problem is," Selma continued, "I don't know much about art theft. Nothing more than the most famous cases, and I haven't thought of them in years. Do you want me to find you someone more knowledgeable?"

"Maybe, but I doubt it. By famous cases, you mean like the theft of the *Mona Lisa* from the Louvre in 1911, or the Isabella Stewart Gardner robbery?"

"That's the idea. There are a few more of that order, though not quite as dramatic or, as with the Gardner Museum, as disastrous. Everyone in Boston has followed that case; the pictures have never been recovered."

"Tell me about the other cases."

"Let me think. Art thefts in America became recognized as an important crime only in the 1970s, I think. If you're writing a paper about this, you must check everything I say. I'm just rattling on, without much to rattle on about."

"I'm not going to publish a word on the subject," Kate assured her. "Probably, as you talk, more examples will come to mind. It always seems to work that way; surely you've noticed."

"Let's see." Selma looked at the ceiling. They were drinking coffee; Selma got up to refill their cups, and then sat down and began to ponder. One of the things Kate liked best about Selma—and Kate liked much about Selma—was that she was not an obsessive questioner, nor one who felt compelled to relate every conversation to herself. She was, rather, able to pick up on a conversation or subject and treat it with seriousness and, if that mood suited the topic under discussion, with a kind of giddy pleasure.

"I think it was in the early 1970s that art theft became a federal crime," Selma said. "You could be sent to prison or fined, or both, if stolen art was taken across state lines. The point, of course, was to get the FBI involved in pursuing stolen art. If the robbery was done for money, the robbers were likelier to be caught. Often they were common crooks without much knowledge of art, who thought this was an easy way to make some dough. It was when the criminals knew what they were doing that recovery became more difficult and sometimes impossible, particularly if they, or the people they steal for, have no intention of selling. Someone who steals a painting for the sheer joy of owning it in secret is almost impossible to catch."

"Ah," Kate said.

Selma waited for further comment, and then, when there was none, went on. "There are also the jokers; these are the stories about art theft that everyone knows; thefts for a joke or to show it could be done. In these cases, the paintings or whatever are usually recovered or returned. Sometimes art students have stolen paintings to copy them, more often in Europe, or to remove the effects of restoration and then return them with a nasty note."

"They sound like the type who used to sit on flagpoles or swallow live goldfish; college pranks for the hell of it," Kate said.

"That's the idea, but art theft is usually serious; very serious, and for money. Here again the art work is usually recovered. You and I steal a Vermeer, let us say; never mind how. We know it's worth millions of dollars. So we send off a note saying for ten percent of its worth, we'll return the picture. There's no way anyone could sell a Vermeer, and we, the thieves, know it. So we're just speaking here of kidnapping and ransom. No one likes to admit it, but both the museums (or owners or galleries) and the insurance companies would far rather get the picture back than help the police or the FBI to prosecute the thieves. Is any of this helping?"

"I'm hanging on every word. Surely what you're describing isn't only ransom, it's also blackmail."

"Right you are. The insurance companies are being blackmailed. But the sad truth is that many museums don't carry insurance on particular paintings or objects; the Gardner didn't. Kate, I do hope you aren't thinking of taking up a life of crime; you don't contemplate trying to steal a painting, do you?" Selma actually sounded a bit worried.

"Absolutely not. Do go on."

"I don't think I can dredge up much more."

"It doesn't sound as though security is very sophisticated in most of the museums that were robbed."

"That's improved. Some of the worst crimes were in Europe decades ago—that notorious theft of Goya's portrait of the Duke of Wellington, for instance, and a Rembrandt that was stolen from the Rijksmuseum in Amsterdam by an insane man and mostly destroyed; security has improved since then. Guards stand about, visitors have to check their belongings, and the press is not given much information about how thefts are carried out, information that might inspire others to similar acts. Technology has become very sophisticated, of course. My museum has circuit television, video cameras, electric beams that follow all movement, and so forth, but even these devices can be evaded by clever thieves. I recently saw a movie with Sean Connery about such

127

cleverly planned thefts. And there have been security systems so sensitive that they respond to the most innocent circumstances, and thus are in danger of being ignored, like the boy who cried wolf. The Gardner, of course, didn't even have separate alarms for each picture or object; I don't know how many museums do. Worst of all, the police and the museum are after different aims: the police want to respond to the alarm and catch the thieves; the museum wants the alarm to scare the thieves away."

"Do thefts still go on?"

"Oh yes. There are often insiders helping thieves, selling information about security systems or helping the criminals to get in after hours, or to stay after hours. Labor is expensive, and guard jobs are boring. Often most of the guards in a museum aren't on the museum's staff at all, or only a few of them are, and these are not highly paid. The greater number of guards are hired from 'cops for rent' or some such organization. Does any of this help?"

"Yes, it does. I can't tell you exactly why, at least not yet, but I can say that what you have told me is important for one main reason: there is a distinction between art theft for profit and art theft in the service of a particular passion. Knowing that is important to me."

"If you say so, Kate. As long as the particular passion doesn't include destroying the picture, as with the Rembrandt." Selma rose and picked up the coffee cups. "Is cheese and bread and salad sufficient for lunch, or shall we go out and celebrate this reunion with something special?" she asked.

"Might we do the something special for dinner? Bread and cheese is a favorite of mine."

"So I remembered. Crusty, fresh French bread, Brie, and Stilton."

"What a memory you have."

"You came to my house only once before I moved to Boston, and that was what I had. You liked it."

"Perhaps we could visit your museum," Kate said, embarrassed as always to hear herself complimented, even by implication. "I'm not much on museums, or art if it comes to that—too visual I guess—but there is an intense pleasure in viewing museum pictures in the company of an informed guide."

"So you shall."

"Good," Kate said. "It has been, and promises to continue to be, a lovely day. I'm glad I decided to stay for all of it."

"Me, too," Selma said.

And Kate promised herself to return one day soon to tell Selma the reasons for her inquiries. Today, Kate needed to speak of other things.

*Not mine own fears, nor the
  prophetic soul
Of the wide world dreaming
  on things to come
Can yet the lease of my true
  love control,
Supposed as forfeit to a con-
  fin'd doom.*

Thirteen

As IT TURNED out, Kate had to wait an hour in the airport. The shuttle flight she had planned to take, in time for which Selma had dropped her off, had been canceled, ostensibly for mechanical problems; actually, Kate had no doubt, because there was an insufficient number of passengers. Airplane travel in the United States had become an experience similar to what Kate had heard of the Army: hurry up, wait, face frustration as a way of life.

Yet she was not sorry to sit in the airport—alas it was not quiet; the blaring of televisions could not be escaped, but by putting in ear plugs, which she always carried when traveling by air, she was able to mute the sound and, as Virginia Woolf put it, let herself down into her mind.

She had not told Selma about Jay, or that she had discovered the truth about who her father was. Only to Leslie had she been able to speak of this event, and she would probably not be able to discuss it even with Leslie today. Selma and Kate had spoken of families, of memories, of loyalty—was it owed to one's near relations, and if so, why, and how much? Kate's contemporaries, including Leslie, had mentioned the lack of attention offered by one's grown children, except in a crisis or if requested, but Leslie was ready enough to concede that one's own lack of deep affection for one's mother hardly suggested the broadest scope of filial attention. Leslie considered herself to have been a better mother than her own mother had been, but surely all mothers thought that.

Selma, now nearing forty, had with her husband decided against having children. As she explained to Kate, she had neither respect nor love for her parents, why continue the pattern? She did not particularly like children—nor did Kate, particularly— and surely one could feel free to choose wisely in the matter of giving birth to them. They both agreed that the pressure to choose motherhood was powerful, but it was avoidable if one knew one's own mind.

"Which many don't," Kate had said. "Or, at a relatively late age, they decide that something vital will be missed. They long to give birth; they do not consider the guilt, the anxiety, the responsibility, the sense of betrayal that may lie ahead and often does."

"My parents," Selma had answered, "who treated us children as impostors, particularly me and my sister because we were not boys, would never have admitted to not wanting children."

"I expect being rich made a difference in my family's case," Kate had said. "One had built-in

131

child care; there was no need to arrange for it constantly in a world ill-adapted to the concept of child care."

"And you were the first girl, with three older brothers. You must have been very welcome."

And Kate thought now, sitting in the airport, that she had been welcome, by her father as welcoming as he could be because she was a girl, by her mother because she was the child of passion. Why had she, Kate, never thought about this? Indeed, how little she had thought of during all those years except her determination to get along in the present and escape in the future into a different world, a world of ideas, and intellect, and poetry; it had been poetry she had relished as a youngster. Perhaps the reason she could not describe anyone, did not register the looks or clothing or body of those she encountered, was that she had not only failed to do this as a child, but had learned not to let such impressions in, only to tolerate and, as far as possible, ignore them.

Jay's appearance (an odd word to choose, she thought, since she did not mean appearance in that sense, she meant emergence, manifestation) had somehow thrust her back into that world of nonobservance. Might she not have noticed something odd, something not quite ordinary, had she looked about her? Was there the residue of passion to be detected, the sense of not belonging to be questioned, her differences from her brothers, looks apart, to be inferred? True, she had turned out not to notice appearances, but had she, on the other hand, turned to detection, or been enticed into it? Was that the result of a dormant sense of something wrong, something hidden?

And so she mused, until the next plane was ready, its wish to welcome passengers announced with sham apologies for the delay. Kate boarded, and managed to quell her introspections and pay attention to the book she had brought for reading on the plane. It demanded her attention and she received it; unlike most travelers, Kate did not prefer light reading on planes; light reading, she liked to admit to Reed, was what she enjoyed when she was pleasantly tired, or ought unquestioningly to be doing something else.

The flight was quick, as shuttle flights always were. Kate headed for the taxi line, to be intercepted by Reed, who had called Selma to ask what plane Kate would be on.

"But you must have had to wait an hour," Kate said, covering her delight at seeing him.

"One always expects to wait at airports; surely you've noticed that."

"I'm beginning to think there is far too much I have never noticed," Kate said. "You have left Jay alone."

"At his urging. He talked to me; he wants to talk to you. And I have come up with the beginnings of a plan. But that can wait until we are home. Let's get a taxi."

"Do you think the taxi driver presents a danger if we talk in his cab?" Kate asked, laughing.

"I'm taking no chances. I'm glad you're back. But I warn you; I think Jay wants to continue his discussion with you about love. You know, in connection with that movie *Brief Encounter*."

"I fear the man's a bloody romantic," Kate said.

"Of course he is; surely you've figured that out by now."

When Kate, back home, looked in on Jay he was lying on the cot almost as she had left him. But now he was awake.

"Reed tells me you want to talk about love," she said.

"Just to finish that conversation."

"You were calling me a cynic."

"Quite right, too."

"As I remember," Kate said, "you were saying that, like that man in the film, you had promised to love all your life. You believe in lifelong love."

"And you said they could promise lifelong love because they would never see each other again. The remark of a cynic."

"I'm not the least cynical. I don't think any couple who live together go on loving in the same way. They love, but differently; the love grows, and changes, and, above all, becomes familiar. Life isn't a movie, Jay."

"You are your mother's daughter; that was more or less her point of view."

"Is that what she said when she refused to run off with you?"

"Not exactly. I don't think she would have claimed for a single minute that she had ever loved Fansler, or ever would. But she refused to believe that love could last in the face of too little money and no social life."

"You're still angry that she didn't run off, after all these years." It was unclear if this was a statement or a question.

"She wouldn't, in the end, give up her social life, which I found empty and silly and so, I'm sure, did she. But she was certain that love couldn't protect you from isolation and the lack of her kind of familiar social events, no chance to welcome people into your home and treat them graciously."

"She did have three sons."

"She'd have left them in a minute, believe me. She'd have left Fansler. What she couldn't leave was the life she had—the life money could buy and old acquaintances could fill. We would have taken you with us. You would have been enough future for her; she didn't need the three sons."

"Have you ever thought—forgive me if this sounds unkind—that your love might not have endured if you had remained together all your life?"

"You think it has endured because I lost it?"

"I only ask."

"How can I answer that, Kate? I've had a whole other life. I've had a wife and stepsons and a satisfactory profession."

"With just a taste of crime to season it. Sorry, that was unkind and unnecessary."

"I gather you don't know much about art theft."

"I know more than I did when last we met; I've learned that stealing art for reasons other than profit is safest for the thief but not always for the art."

Jay appeared to ignore this. "I have odd, I suppose dated, ideas of love and truth and honor," he said. "I believed, and still believe, that if you love someone, you cling to them. If you learn that a beloved object has been stolen and sold, you help to recover it. If you know someone who has murdered

135

and who you suspect will murder again, you speak out against him. The conclusions of a romantic, you will say, and you are right. It is that romantic strain, what's more, that has brought me here, to your home, to endanger you and your husband."

"Reed has some thoughts about that; he's going to tell me what they are; then, if I agree, he'll tell you."

"Whatever his thoughts, I'm not going to stay here after today. I've decided. I wanted to meet you before I died, and then, again in danger of being killed, I ran to you. You've every right to call it romantic. Except that scientists, evolutionists, are telling us today that it's our genes that matter to us, the search for immortality in our offspring. Perhaps that is what seemed to urge me to find you: onward with my genes."

"Not too onward; as you now know, I have no children. The last of my line, if that matters. I can't say the thought of my genes, such as they are, ending here, has ever troubled me. As it happens, I spoke with the friend I was visiting in Boston about people like her, like me, who do not feel that almost universal longing for children. I hope you were not searching for immortality in your progeny when you set out to find me."

"No. I'm a different sort of romantic. Evolution is a fascinating subject, but not one, in my view, to be taken seriously. Genes aren't passed on like a baton in a relay race. Had you had children, they might have got the genes of someone generations, even centuries back. It was you I wanted to find, Kate, not anyone beyond you."

* * *

When Reed and Kate sat down to confer about their situation, which seemed to Kate to grow tenser with each day and to become, each day, no nearer to a solution, Reed delivered the news of his discoveries.

"I hired a very pricey detective who works in the area of Jay's hometown," Reed said. "I learned a number of facts about his origins. They're intriguing facts but hardly useful ones. What it amounts to in summary is this: Jay—which we might as well go on calling him—was born—"

"What do you mean," Kate interrupted, "by saying you 'learned a number of facts'? You just make a phone call and someone scurries around and behold, you know all about whomever you care to investigate?"

"More or less," Reed said. "There is no privacy in today's world; it is best to accept that fact. We needn't approve of it, or welcome it, but privacy as we knew it is a thing of the past. Between the Web and a good private inquiry agent there's little that can't be discovered about someone, from birth to death, and including one's financial and medical history among other things."

"That's a horrible thought," Kate said.

"I agree. Someday something may be done about it; a code may be developed that is impenetrable. But there has never been a code that couldn't be broken, sooner or later. For the moment, however, perhaps we better deal with the problem immediately before us."

Kate sighed and nodded. "What I discovered," Reed continued, "is that Jay's real name, his birth name, is Edmund M. Dyson, which is the name under which he went to Yale's architecture school, and

the name he used when he was forming the firm
that he is still a partner in, though an inactive one."

"But wasn't he afraid my mother or someone
might find him if he used his real name, the name
she knew him by?"

"You forget, my dear. Your mother had no desire
to find him; the other Fanslers didn't know of his
existence."

"And what of Jay Ebenezer Smith?" Kate asked.

"That is the name, or close to the name (we may
never know exactly how the Witness Protection
Program deals with these matters) under which he
hid out and entered into a new life."

"So Ebenezer had nothing to do with his parents'
love of Dickens?"

"Yes, it did, oddly enough. His mother died when
he was a young child; his father was a hard-
working accountant who lived either for figures or
Dickens, whose novels he read and reread all his
life. No doubt, when not reading Dickens, he did
his best for his son after his wife's death."

"How on earth did your pricey detective find all
that out?"

"Not hard. Jay's father worked as an accountant
and was a member of a Dickens' society. He seems
to have had no other interests except, one hopes,
Jay. He did, at any rate, attend PTA meetings at Jay's
school."

Kate stared at Reed.

"Well," Reed said, "it is a little more complicated
than I was going to bother you with right now; time
presses. I promise, you would have eventually had
every tiny detail if and when you wanted it. When
Jay married, which he did while in the Witness Pro-

tection Program, he showed his new wife and her sons the papers and materials of any sort he had been allowed to take with him into his new life; no photographs were allowed, for obvious reasons. The papers he was allowed to keep were his father's, from which all those with names had been removed. These papers bore ample evidence of the father's interests and work. The detective I hired visited the sons of Jay's wife, now dead, and was shown those papers. The sons, by the way, know now that Jay was in the Witness Protection Program when he lived with them, and that he took a different name when he left the program. They have seen him since; I gather theirs is a cordial relationship, not that that matters as far as we are concerned."

"Why did he use his made-up name when he met us?"

"You'll have to ask him. But there's no doubt the Ebenezer was a nod to his father's memory. It's true, by the way, as he told you the first time you met, that his mother drank. She was an alcoholic who killed herself and Jay's older brother; that was in the police records; she was driving while intoxicated. Like many children of alcoholics, even ones who did not kill themselves or anybody else, Jay has never been a drinker, at least as far as records show."

"And as we mentioned before," Kate said, "he might have chosen Ebenezer because Scrooge reformed. I somehow think the whole question of reformation has always been on his mind."

"True, no doubt. But it hardly helps us to decide what to do about him now."

"I'm working on that," Reed said. "Pondering

and planning. Will you wait until tomorrow to hear my proposal?"

"You are remembering that Clara comes on Tuesday."

"Ah, yes. I meant to ask you if we might not, this once, postpone Clara to a later day in the week, or cancel this week. Since we have never canceled her before, I think a postponement is preferable. Will you call her or shall I?"

"I'll call her," Kate said.

Kate was torn between insisting that Reed tell her his plans this very moment and the knowledge that she had classes tomorrow as well as other preparations that could hardly wait. She was, in addition, scheduled tomorrow to attend a lecture by a visiting Shakespearean scholar whose work she ought to at least review in her mind, however sketchily.

*You know my father hath no
child but I,
Nor more is like to have.*

Fourteen

KATE DID NOT attend all the lectures sponsored by her department, nor even a majority of them. She had, however, read the works of this speaker, and admired particularly his book on what he called "Shakespeare's comedies of forgiveness." These were Shakespeare's late plays; they were often violent in action and complicated in plot; they were not among his most popular or most frequently performed works, and yet they held a particular fascination for certain critics of Shakespeare, among whom today's lecturer was prominent.

Kate settled into her seat anticipating a certain pleasure in listening to this scholar, but without any marked expectations. She had just dug out a notebook, located her pen, and prepared herself to listen with attention when she was shocked into a state of stunning awareness. The man was speaking of fathers and daughters, of their role in these late plays, and of the centrality of the father-daughter bond.

There were lovers in these plays, he said, whose separation and reunion was central to the story. But it has not always been noted how few if any daughters in Shakespeare can be said to encounter their lovers without at the same time being closely involved in a struggle with their fathers; it is as though the lover is but a surrogate for the daughter's bond to her father, and his to her. This, while a more minor point in *Othello* (Desdemona's father warns Othello: "she has deceived her father and may thee") is overwhelmingly present in the late plays. There, the daughters are essential to their fathers' redemption. The fathers, cruel or dangerously undiscerning, ultimately achieve forgiveness only through their daughters. The daughters are often banished, or banish themselves in search of the lovers their fathers have brutally rejected; it is only in the rediscovery of these daughters that the fathers are redeemed.

The lecturer continued in this vein, discussing *Cymbeline*, *The Winter's Tale*, *The Tempest*, and perhaps others. Kate had stopped listening closely, and was awakened from her reverie by a question from the audience, most of them students, some faculty. "Isn't *Lear* one of the best examples of your theory?" a student asked.

"Certainly," was the answer. "A prime example. I did not allude to it since Cordelia and the end of *Lear* are so well known to us, as the late plays are not. *Lear* is a tragedy, and Cordelia pays for her father's earlier arrogance and newfound sanity with her life. In the late plays to which I wished to call attention the prevalence of this theme is paramount; in the late comedies, that is, the daughter and the plot that surrounds her encompass the whole process of redemption. These plays are, of course, called comedies because they end happily, not because they are humorous or trivial or farcical." There were other questions, but Kate had tuned out.

She had been invited—ordered would be the more accurate word—to attend the dinner always offered a lecturer. She had intended to duck off from the dinner if there were a sufficient number of diners— that is, members of the department—available, but she changed her mind. Offered a seat immediately to the right of the lecturer, she accepted it willingly; this was not always the case. The deference one paid to lecturers in these circumstances did not lead to animated conversation. Rather, the lecturer seemed inclined to continue holding forth. But Kate was eager to speak with this man. She waited until he had ordered a drink and his dinner before engaging him in conversation. The male faculty member to the lecturer's left was in any case explaining in some detail his own interpretation of the late comedies.

With some relief, Kate thought, the lecturer turned to her. She told him how much she had enjoyed, indeed been enlightened, by his lecture (or the part I heard, she said inwardly) and asked if he thought that daughters today, or in the modern world altogether, could be said to play, or to have played, a similar part in the redemption of their fathers. In contemporary or recent literature did fathers ever feel reclaimed by daughters, or was this ultimately a metaphor rather than a reality, and not a modern metaphor at all?

"An interesting question," he said. "I have read stories from the last century and this in which

143

daughters do redeem the father. But it is less powerful, and lacks Shakespeare's incisive use of metaphor.
The daughter, I don't like to say represents, but she
does stand in for, she enables, the father to receive
grace, to pass into a state of grace. Whether in what
we call 'real life' that ever happens is doubtful, but
not impossible. The power of the daughter's role
in regard to the father, however, is definitely meta-
phoric; it is always literary, I suspect, rather than
actually enacted in the world. Which is another
way of saying that 'real life' is so complex, so complicated, that the dramatic essence of what has occurred is rarely perceived."

"Suppose," Kate said, "one were to write a story
where the father felt impelled to search out a daughter he had lost or perhaps never known, somewhat
as in *The Winter's Tale*. Might the author be able,
though only feebly in comparison with Shakespeare's
plays, to suggest that while the father sought his
daughter, he was really, though unconsciously, seek-
ing redemption, forgiveness for other blunders in
his life?"

"Is what you mean that he wished for grace, but
did not know how to seek it and, in ignorance of the
actual object of his search, pursued the lost daughter as what we might call an instinctive substitute?
I'm afraid I haven't put that very clearly."

"I think it's very clear," Kate said, "and I thank
you for a most illuminating lecture. I look forward
to reading it when it is published." And she turned
to the person on her right, whom she had been
rather assiduously ignoring. She was not, even now,
willing to lend a conscientious ear, but she would
listen as far as courtesy demanded. Knowing the

man, she doubted that he would perceive the exact quality of her attention. Part of her mind was free to think about the question of daughters as metaphor.

For reasons she could not explain even to herself, Kate did not tell Reed about the lecture or the dinner conversation with the lecturer. It seemed to Kate that he had appeared as an oracle, a soothsayer, and that she needed to digest his message. Reed, on the other hand, had had an idea about Kate's mother.

"Has it ever occurred to you that she might have left some evidence behind, some reference in a diary or appointment book, whatever, of her affair with Jay?"

"No," Kate said. "She left me her pearls and a ring my father—I mean her husband—had given her on some anniversary, I forget which one. The ring is in the safe-deposit box at the bank; I wear the pearls, as you may have noticed."

"Of course I've noticed. Did you ever ask if she left any papers, and private memoranda—that sort of thing?"

"Really, Reed, this sounds like all those detective stories where evidence turns up at the last minute, because nobody had thought to look for it before, or if they knew of it, to bother mentioning it to anyone. Do you really think I'm going to find something of importance at the top of a closet somewhere? And where?"

"Why not ask Laurence? It can't hurt. As I remember, you said you didn't want anything of hers when she died, except the pearls and the ring. You just turned your back."

145

"That's putting it rather harshly. My brothers all had homes and could use furnishings and so forth; their wives could use anything of my mother's they wanted. I didn't think there was anything there that I could use at the time. You make it sound as though I just tidied my mother away. Well, maybe I did. She had been ill, and we hadn't been what you could call close for a long time."

"I meant no recriminations, and justifications are not called for. Why don't you just give Laurence a call. After all, he's perfectly aware of the latest events which do evoke certain questions about your mother."

"And while I'm calling Laurence, will you be preparing to tell me your plan? I'll postpone Clara, but we have got to get Jay out of here, preferably without getting him killed in the process."

"Don't postpone Clara. I've almost worked out a plan. Give me till tomorrow, please, Kate."

"All right. But you do realize that we haven't kept secrets or plans or cogitations from each other before. You don't think Jay's having a sadly negative effect on our relationship?"

"No, I don't. It's an unusual circumstance, and will not end in my keeping anything from you. Go call Laurence. I'm going to take Banny for a walk."

Laurence, upon being asked about their mother's "personal effects"—the term Kate had come up with for what she was after—immediately turned Kate over to his wife. This sort of question was in a wife's domain; Janice would know if there were any of his mother's personal effects around, and if so, where they were. Kate called Janice, not without some misgivings. She and Janice had never taken to each other. Put more bluntly, they had disliked each other from the moment they met; their ideas were utterly disparate, their values at opposite ends of any spectrum of values. An absolute break had been avoided only by their mutual refusal to let it happen, never to remain together long enough for any disruptive subject to rear its head and set off a confrontation.

Janice, however, by now having learned of Jay's amazing appearance in their lives, and imagining Kate's horror at discovering her mother's infidelity, was not inclined to make difficulties about this present request. Apart from furnishings and personal belongings, Janice told Kate, Louise had left a set of notebooks which she, Janice, would retrieve from their storage room in the basement if Kate cared to come over and examine them. Janice frankly admitted she had no idea why she had kept them, except that Laurence did not seem happy about throwing away any of his mother's possessions. Did Kate want to come tomorrow afternoon when Janice would have brought them up from the basement?

Kate suggested that tomorrow afternoon both she and Janice could descend to the basement; there Janice might leave Kate to examine the notebooks. If Kate did not wish to borrow them, they could then be left in the storage room; no need to bring them up to the apartment. They would certainly, at the very least, be dusty.

And so it was settled. Kate had been fairly sure that Janice would not wish to hang about the basement, and she was right. The box containing the notebooks was found; one of the porters in the basement helped Kate to get them down. The box was indeed dusty, though, to Kate's relief, not nibbled by rats. Janice left.

Kate had no idea what she could expect to find. The notebooks were nicely bound volumes with blank pages on which their owner, presumably, was free to write poetry, a diary, or an explosive narrative in code. Each book had a date on its first page. Kate took up the earliest. Its date was some years before Kate was born; had Louise met Jay yet? If not in this notebook, perhaps in a slightly later one.

Kate turned to the first page on which Louise had written. What she found was an account of a dinner party; its date, its menu, its guests, and what Louise had worn. Well, Kate thought, if one gave dinner parties, perhaps one needed to record what was served, what one wore, who attended. Otherwise, Kate supposed, one might commit the frightful social gaffe of giving guests the same food to eat as they had been given the last time they came.

Kate turned the pages. Each page recorded the details of a dinner party; occasionally of a cocktail party; each page was the same, in format and in subject. Kate put that notebook down, and looking through other notebooks, all of which appeared to have identical entries, found one the year of her birth. This notebook was in no way different from the others. There was a record of a birthday party for William, Kate's middle brother, listing the games played, the favors given, the children asked. Otherwise, it was all dinner and cocktail parties.

Kate took each notebook from the box and examined it. There was nothing else, no paper with writing on it between the notebook pages, no indication that what was here had provided its author with anything but details about occasions of entertainment. Not even the weather was worthy of note.

Kate slowly returned the notebooks to the box, arranging them in their original order; there were often several years covered in one notebook, and the last of them, from the year when Louise fell ill, was mostly vacant. There was a last dinner party of Louise's life, and that was that. Kate beckoned to the porter, who put the box back where it had been stored; Kate went upstairs to thank Janice.

"Did you find anything of interest?" Janice asked.

"No," Kate said. "Only details about dinner parties."

"What sort of details?"

"What was served; what she wore; who came."

"Well, of course she kept a record of that. It's only sensible, if you entertain a lot. Wasn't there anything else?"

"No. That was all. Did she leave any other writing that you know of?"

"Nothing. I remember Laurence and David looked to see if she had written any special letters when they were born, letters that might have been returned to her. Nothing. She wasn't a writer, you know. She was a proper lady, a good hostess. I really can't believe this about, you know, your 'father.' I just can't believe it."

"Before DNA, we would have been free to disbelieve it," Kate said. "I find the facts about this romance as unlike my mother as you do, but she

149

was my mother and Jay was my father. If you notice, I don't really look like my brothers."

"I noticed that long ago. You didn't act like them either. But the fact that you were female seemed to explain it all—plus the dreadful times then, of course, which encouraged the worst in young people, and still do. What's become of your father by the way?"

"We aren't quite sure," Kate said, she hoped not too untruthfully. She could hardly tell Janice that Jay was hiding out in their maid's room. Well, she could hardly tell anybody.

"Thank you for letting me see the notebooks," Kate said. "If you don't want to be bothered keeping them, probably some library would be interested in that record of what was served by hostesses of Louise's class at that time."

"I'll ask Laurence about it," Janice said. And with that Kate left, politely refusing the offer of tea.

Kate needed two drinks before she could bring herself to hold forth about the contents of her mother's notebooks.

"What did you expect to find?" Reed asked when he had heard her out. "What did you hope to find? A journal recording her passion and its renunciation; the birth of her lover's child?"

"I can't believe she's my mother. That's the answer. Jay got some other woman with child and dumped it on my mother."

"If you will calm down and think a minute," Reed said, "you will recall that we also tested Laurence to be assured that he and you had the same
150

mother. I fear there will be no surprises in 'the dark backward and abysm of time.' You better be impressed; that's one of the three quotations from Shakespeare I know by heart."

"What are the other two?" Kate could not help asking.

" 'Dressed in a little brief authority'; I think of that at least three times a day. Also 'the readiness is all.' " As I was saying, the solution to the problem occupying our maid's room is not in the 'dark backward and abysm of time,' but very much present, now, immediate."

"For which you have a plan."

"I do. And you shall hear it. But I'm wrong. I do have another Shakespearean quotation. 'Men have died, and worms have eaten them, but not for love.' "

"You may be wrong about that, when it comes to Jay," Kate said.

"And so your mother, to keep from dying of love, went on with her scheduled social life as she had always done, to keep regret, longing, misery at bay. Do not be too hard on your mother."

"Maybe," Kate said. "I don't think she was wrong not to run off with Jay. I've told him so; love which is not tested by time and extreme proximity lasts far better. And she was good at the life she led, particularly now that Jay had provided the only thing she had lacked: physical passion. No, I don't blame her for not abandoning the life she knew and was good at. I don't know what I'm sad about. I guess I hoped for something written, something testifying to the experience she had had."

"What you mean," Reed said, "is that you wish

Edith Wharton's mother had written Edith Wharton's novels."

"Touché," Kate said.

*Imagination gives to any
nothing
A local habitation and a name.*

Fifteen

E ARLY THE NEXT morning Reed, who usually
walked Banny at that time, suggested to Kate
that she come along, too. Kate, who drinking coffee
and reading the *New York Times* was sunk in her
usual and necessary solitude for that time of day,
stared at Reed in startled bewilderment.

"Please," he said. He had put on his Irish hat, as
he called it, a brimmed tweed favorite that could be
crushed in a pocket, drowned in a storm, and still
retain its gentlemanly insouciance.

"Since when have you taken to wearing a hat for
Banny's walks?" Kate asked. "Have you been feeling chilly about the head?"

"The last few days," Reed said, ignoring the last
part of the question. "Are you coming?"

With a sigh, Kate abandoned her coffee and the
paper, catching in Reed's tone a sense of urgency.

When they had reached the park, and released
Banny from her leash, as was legal before nine in

153

the morning—although, unlike most dogs, Banny rarely wandered far away from them, or (illegally) pursued squirrels—Reed told Kate his plan.

"Tomorrow morning," he said, "this same trio—man, woman, and dog—shall set out on this walk. Only, the man won't be me. He will be Jay, wearing my hat and a pair of glasses like mine. You and he will walk and talk exactly as we are walking and talking now. The idea, if you haven't guessed, is that he will be taken for me."

"I had got that far," Kate said. "And where will you be? Remember, tomorrow is Tuesday; Clara is coming, since you vetoed my postponing her."

"Exactly. I shall be in the maid's room. As we agreed, Clara never goes in there. But if, by some perverse chance, she should go in there, she will find me lying on the cot, ready with a reason for that uncharacteristic exercise."

"Jay and I, meanwhile, will . . . what?"

"You'll keep walking and talking, eventually putting the leash on Banny and wandering over to our local precinct."

"I haven't a clue where it is."

"Of course you haven't. Every citizen should know where her local precinct is, but we'll take that subject up another time. When you get to the precinct, you will ask for a police officer named Ringley."

"As in the circus."

"Not quite. An officer named Ringley who will escort Jay into the interior of the station where he will be locked into and expected to relax in a holding cell. You and Banny will then come home, stopping on your way into the building to mention

154

loudly to the men in the lobby that your husband has had to leave for work."

"Is someone supposed to overhear me say that?"

"I don't know if it will be overheard, or if it will be believed if overheard, but we're doing our best. Have you got it all straight?"

"I suppose it's no good asking where Jay is going after he leaves the holding cell."

"The plan is for him to proceed in a police car, some hours later, to a prison upstate where he will be protected for the time being."

"And what are we, or you, since you seem pretty much to have taken this over without much consultation, going to be doing while Jay is in the cooler?"

"This is consultation; I'm consulting you. True, I arranged the police part before I had consulted you, but time was of the essence."

"You haven't told Jay about this yet?"

"Certainly not; I wanted your agreement or refusal before going any further."

"You apparently assume that you and Jay look enough alike to get away with this charade."

"You've never been great at noticing physical characteristics, for which I have long admired you. They aren't as important as everyone else in our society seems to think. In fact, however, Jay and I are of a height, not dissimilar in coloring or in the way we walk and carry ourselves. If you sign off on this plan, I'll spend a large part of this evening encouraging him to walk like me. If this doesn't work, we haven't lost a great deal. We have to get him out of our apartment, and he'll be safe for a short while with the police."

"And if they, whoever they or he are, spot him the moment we leave the house and nab him, what exactly am I to do?"

"Rush back upstairs and we'll call the police. But I very much hope that won't happen, and I don't think it will. They may not even know that he is in our apartment, but for various reasons to do with certain lurking types I've spotted, I think they do. Now, take my arm."

"What?"

"Take my arm. As though we were out together to have an important talk and needed to feel close."

"We are having an important talk."

"You know perfectly well what I mean—a private, personal talk; we're making up because I treated you badly last night. Take my arm." Kate did so.

"Good," Reed said, squeezing it to him. "Take Jay's arm tomorrow. Even if they see through this plan, they are hardly going to try anything with you hanging on to him, a large dog nearby, and many people in the park and on the streets. That, at least, is my hope."

"Mine, too, Reed," Kate said, squeezing his arm and resting her head for a moment on his shoulder. "You do realize that Freud and his followers could hardly fail to think Oedipus complex; my husband and my father treated with identical familiarity."

"We shall have to risk that interpretation, as I hope you agree."

"But I still want to know the details of who this is who is after Jay, and why, and what sort of person or persons we're up against."

"Jay is going to tell us all about it tonight, under

threat of immediate exposure. But I don't think he'll need the threat to tell us."

"Be sure to leave enough time for his lessons in walking like you."

"Remind me, when this is over, if it ever is over," Reed said, "to tell you again how much I love and admire you."

"And me with a criminal for a father, and the genes of heaven only knows what else seething about."

"You're you. Do try to keep that in mind, will you?"

And they walked on for a bit, Kate's arm in his.

Reestablished in the maid's room that evening, they were seated in their by now familiar position of the men perched on either end of the cot and Kate, on the chair, with her feet extended onto the cot between them. Jay began to recount how this deathly relation between him and his enemy had come about.

"I've already told you some of it," he said.

"So you have," Reed agreed. "But we could do with a bit more elaboration on that part of the story, as well as some description of the man who is determined to kill you."

"I've told you; he became obsessed with me. The FBI told me that, though I hardly needed to be told. He's shadowed me ever since he got out; it was a while before I noticed. Before he wanted me to notice."

"I have trouble putting it together," Reed said. "I mean, the different parts of your life. The architect, partner in a firm famous for its work in restoration, and the young man willing to steal a painting from a gallery, and later, the older man willing to testify against a killer who must have had friends on the outside, even if he was convicted."

"I didn't fear his friends. He hadn't the means to pay enough; he wasn't part of a gang or an organization. No, he was the only one to fear. I sensed what a sick person he was from the first time I met him."

"Why did you go on with it?"

"Why did I agree to help my friend commit theft in the first place? Because it was unjust; because his mother ought to have had her picture. It was hers by rights. The theft didn't seem that terrible, and my friend promised to return the picture one day. And he did."

By this time he was talking to Kate, not by any means excluding Reed, but there could be no doubt who his chosen audience was or to whom the story needed to be told.

"It all goes back to Louise, to your mother. She refused to come away with me—well, I've told you that. There are two bits I neglected to mention. One was that I wanted to take you with me. I had nothing, no one else. Oh, I had fine plans about how it would happen without a scandal. We would pretend you had died, or been kidnapped, or—one mad scheme after another, all impossible, of course. I did see that. But she left me nothing. She had her family, her boys, her damn social life, everything; and what did I have? Well, she offered me money. I knew it wasn't as though she were buying me off—I never thought that, and neither did she. Her argument was that I needed to get started at some

158

profession, she had the money to give, I could pay it back someday, and so forth. I needed the money; of course I did. But I felt she needed to give it to me, and I wanted a part in nothing that would assuage her guilt at deserting me, at throwing me out, at ending it. I knew and she knew that she could just turn away, hide her bruised heart, and go on with her chosen life. I wasn't going to make it easier for her if I could help it. But I certainly needed money. So when the chance to make a good sum, at least for those days, came along . . ."

"The plan to steal the Shakespeare picture for your friend."

"Exactly. I don't know if I mentioned that he offered me money; he'd kept his nose to the grindstone and made a neat packet by then. I needed money badly, as I've said, as Louise knew. I hadn't a penny to my name. I like to think—I certainly persuaded myself then—that if I hadn't been convinced that my friend had a right to get that picture back, if I hadn't resented the picture having been sold from under his mother's nose, I wouldn't have agreed to the whole caper. Sure, I know what you're thinking: that I probably identified the loss of that picture with my loss of your mother; all I can say is I was highly motivated to commit a crime. A victimless crime, as I thought of it."

"Except for the museum that owned the picture," Reed injected.

"Well, they didn't trouble too much to find out who really owned the picture, did they? I don't think museums and galleries and private owners are too particular on that score. Anyway, I didn't even think about the museum then."

159

"And your friend hired this man who helped you to steal the picture."

"That's him. That's the one."

"And he has found some comrades to help him in his quest for you now, is that it?"

"I don't really know. I think so, because the one or two times I've caught sight of him, there seemed to be others. Helpers, I think; hired help. He intended to kill me himself; they were just for the capture is the way I see it."

"And he hates you because you testified against him?"

"He was a rough type, even when we met; I'd asked my friend not to use him, but he wouldn't listen. And, in fact, nothing much went wrong. Not during that theft."

"But later."

"Years later. I read about an art theft he was involved in; they were spotted, and he shot one of the security guards. He didn't need to shoot him; he said when the police spoke to him—eventually it was the FBI—that the guy would have killed him if he hadn't shot first. But the security man didn't have a gun. It became obvious that what he feared was that the guard had seen him, could have described him, would have led to his arrest."

"Surely killing the guard would be as likely to lead to an arrest?" Kate said.

"Not really. He denied being the shooter; he insisted the guy working with him was the one who did the shooting. That seemed unlikely, given the character of his accomplice—no record, and no gun. The bullet from the killer's gun indicated the kind of gun it was, a kind that I knew the man had;

160

he had had it when we did our theft, which was one of the main reasons I didn't like or trust him; I don't like guns. The police couldn't find the gun; he'd ditched it somewhere."

"He'd have got off on insufficient evidence without your testimony, is that it?" Reed asked.

"That, and that the other guy, his accomplice, might have been convicted; there was always that chance."

"So you testified and went into Witness Protection. Why did you take yourself out of it?"

"He'd been given a long enough sentence to assure my safety. After a time, I wanted to get on with my life. I wanted to get back to being an architect."

"If I've got this straight," Kate said, "the robbery in which this man killed a guard happened twenty years or so after the art theft you took part in."

"That's right."

"And you'd married the woman with the two sons in the meantime."

"Yes. She and the boys—they were small children then—went into the Witness Protection Program with me. I came out alone; the marriage was over by then. I'd adopted the boys; I still see them occasionally; I always kept up with them; my wife died a few years ago."

"And we are to gather that the killer was paroled against all expectations," Reed said.

"When he was convicted, they promised they would fight parole if it came up, appear before the parole board. But it was a different cast of characters twenty years later, I guess. Anyway, he was out, with one aim in mind: to get me."

"And he found out about Kate being your daughter."

"Yes. I never guessed that. But before I heard he was out, he'd taken to—what's the word—stalking me. He knew more about me than I did. I didn't even know he was out on parole until he let me know he was out. When I discovered that he knew who Kate was, I tried disappearing. But he was always there. So I came here to hide, endangering Kate, endangering both of you. It would be hard to think of a more perfect screwup; I know that. I want to get out of here, and get him off your backs at least."

The three of them stood up to stretch their legs, not that there was sufficient room to move about, but the relief of standing was for the moment enough.

"You've never forgiven my mother," Kate said. "Everything you've done, all that you've told us, was about her—was aimed at her. You became a success at your profession, but she had expected that of you; that wasn't sufficient to pay her back. But going to the bad, committing a theft, testifying against a killer, putting your life in danger, then leaving the Witness Protection Program to become the target of a maniac—all that was to make her sorry, wasn't it? She had died somewhere along the way, but by that time it hardly mattered. And then there was me."

Kate had expected Jay to object to this analysis, which in fact she thought a bit oversimplified, but he made no objection, just kept silent.

"Tell me what you want me to do," he then said to Reed.

So Reed explained the plan, while Kate went into the kitchen to make some coffee. Doing this, as she had more often in the last few days than in most of the rest of her life, she was reminded of the English always fixing tea. Although lately, it occurred to her, in contemporary English novels, they served coffee instead. Kate returned to the maid's room to find Reed, his Irish hat on his head, walking and moving as much as was possible in the confined space while Jay watched him and tried to follow his movements. Kate put the tray with the coffee down on the cot and left them to it.

But later that night, she asked Reed why the police in the local precinct and upstate should agree to take Jay into custody, or pretend to.

"You forget how long I was an assistant D.A.," Reed said. "One makes connections, one gets to know people, one asks and returns favors."

"It seems a pretty big favor to me," Kate said.

"It is. It's a pretty big problem we're facing; don't you think so?"

Kate didn't bother to answer, but she pondered, not for the first time, what all this was costing Reed; what it would cost him in the future.

> Look, *with what courteous*
> *action*
> *It waves you to a more re-*
> *moved ground.*

Sixteen

EARLY THE NEXT morning—early at least in the light of Kate's usual day—she and Jay and Banny set out, Jay being, to all appearances, Reed. Kate took his arm, and found herself tempted to discuss this identification of her father with her husband with as many Freudian and Lacanian references as she could muster. But she resisted. Jay, seemingly beyond speech, concentrated on imitating Reed's walk and wearing Reed's Irish hat, efforts which obviously consumed all of his energies. Except that he had mentioned, as they set out, his wish that this walk might be not a performance but a regular father-daughter excursion, there was only silence from Jay.

Kate, graveled for lack of matter, turned to Shakespeare. "Do you know *The Winter's Tale*?" she asked Jay.

"No," he said. "Tell me about it."

"Somehow your appearance in my life reminded

me of *The Winter's Tale*—although our ages are all wrong, and the plot hardly applies. Still, there are echoes."

"Tell me."

"There is this king, Leontes, who is being visited by his boyhood friend, Polixenes, now king of somewhere else. Leontes is a fortunate man: he has a wonderful wife, a small son, another child expected, and this long visit from his friend. Oh, dear. Have you ever thought about how hard it is to tell the plot of a Shakespeare play? His plots are almost as tumultuous as opera plots, but with him it's the language that gets you; with operas I guess it's the music."

Kate was aware that she was chatting on, not making too much sense. The park was full of cars (permitted before ten) and rampant off-the-leash dogs (permitted before nine), along with dogless people hurrying to offices. Kate found it hard to imagine that anyone was watching them.

"Go on with the plot," Jay said.

"For no reason anyone can fathom, Leontes decides his friend and wife are having an affair. He expels his wife from the court; he may even order her to be killed. His son, meanwhile, has died of sorrow; his wife has given birth to a daughter supposed to be Polixenes' (it was a long visit); he orders the baby to be killed also; the friend makes a hasty exit. They send to the Delphic oracle, who says Leontes was all wrong; his friend and his wife never dallied with one another. Twenty years pass. The son of the friend, Polixenes, meets Perdita, the not-killed daughter who lives with her supposed father, a shepherd. They fall in love and make their way

165

back to the court. The wife, Hermione, turns out not to have died but to have been preserved by means that would be invaluable to the cosmetic industry if they could bottle it; the friend's son replaces the lost son, the daughter lives. I know it sounds mad, but the language is heavenly. As to the plot, I haven't a clue why it comes to mind. Except that a lost daughter is found. She is, however, seventeen or so and gorgeous."

"Also, there is a lot of sudden, but lasting anger."

"Yes, that too."

Kate fastened Banny's leash to her collar, and they made their way out of the park and toward the street.

"I left something out," Kate said. "And it's important. The traduced wife, Hermione, had a good friend, Paulina, who has defended her and stood by her all those years. She is rewarded at the play's end with a new husband, since her first one has been killed in Polixenes' service: he famously exits 'pursued by bear.' Pauline says she will, like an old turtle—I think she means turtledove—go off to lament her lost husband. But Leontes simply gives her another husband. All the loose ends must be tied up for the finale, if it's a comedy. Shakespeare was unusually good on women's friendships, most of the time."

"You say that the play makes you think of me, of us?"

"Not really. But there are certain echoes. Since we are not actors, we have let fifty years, rather than twenty, pass."

Jay seemed inclined to speak, and then did not.

"Oh, well," Kate said, "there's one thing to be

said for Shakespeare's plots and opera plots: telling them certainly takes time. We're almost at the police station."

"Do you know what Reed plans after this little charade we've been performing; after I am safely in the arms of the police?"

"No; I'm not sure he does. But perhaps one day we will sit again, as we sat in Laurence's club, and by the sailing pond, and simply converse."

"The thing about Leontes in the play," Jay said, "is that he was a king and could make all things come right. I can't imagine what Shakespeare would do with our plot; I only hope Reed will do something beneficent."

The three of them, Kate, Jay, Banny, walked into the police station. The man at the desk seemed, rather to Kate's surprise, to know who they were and why they were there. (Kate, though she was rather ashamed of it, had no great opinion of the police.) She and Banny left before she could get involved in any conversations with anyone: Reed's instructions; she waved goodbye to Jay. Walking home on the busy streets, she and Banny met with no incident whatever.

At home, Kate greeted Clara. Clara did not mention the maid's room, and before their usual exchange could get under way, the telephone rang. Kate answered; it was Leslie.

"I was just thinking of you," Kate said.

"Really? And why was that?"

"I was thinking of Paulina in *The Winter's Tale.*"

"I'm an artist, Kate, not a literary type. Paulina is, I'm to gather, a good friend."

"Yes. Like Rosalind and Celia. All right, never mind. It's been a frantic few days. I shall tell you about it soon. Meanwhile, I'm neither here nor there."

"Still brooding about the effects of your new discovery about your father?"

"I haven't had much time to brood. I'm hoping you'll be able to give me many hours to talk about all this, and to figure out what I feel about it all. I, who always know what I feel, haven't a clue."

"That means the clue is so obvious you've overlooked it. I'll clear the decks for you anytime you're ready. Am I to meet the proud new father?"

"Perhaps. Somehow I doubt it."

"Why? Am I insufficiently presentable?"

"I doubt he'll be around to be presented. But one day, who knows?"

And Kate went on to ask about Leslie's life and work; these were always fraught with tension and the stuff of spellbinding narration. When Kate had said goodbye to Leslie and hung up, she went in search of Clara, who was just beginning one of her thorough jobs on the bedroom. Having greeted Clara, Kate decided to risk a soft knock on the maid's room door.

But even as she approached the door, Reed emerged through it. "Is Clara in the bedroom?" he asked.

Kate nodded.

"Good," Reed said. And he walked out to the entrance hall, opened and noisily shut their front door and shouted: "I got away unexpectedly early. Is Clara here? I'll try not to get in her way. I'm just going to say hello to Clara." And he vanished toward the bedroom.

Kate went back into the kitchen to make more coffee. These early mornings are getting to me, she thought, and no amount of caffeine can make up for too-early risings. Reed joined her in a few minutes. Once the coffee was ready, they repaired to the living room, always the last room Clara cleaned on her weekly visits.

"I take it it all went well," Reed said.

"Very well. I didn't even have to go far enough into the police station to explain Banny. Now will you please tell me your next move—that is, if you have any idea what it is."

"At least Jay is safe for now and out of here; do give me credit for that."

"Consider yourself credited. How long will the police keep him?"

At that moment the house phone sounded. Puzzled, for one hardly expects visitors in the middle of the morning, and unanticipated visitors were hardly likely to appear at any time, Reed went to answer it.

"It's your brother Laurence," he said, returning to the living room.

"Laurence!" Kate exclaimed, as though Reed had announced a camel driver with beast in tow. "Laurence has never been here, I don't think."

"I don't think I've ever been here," Laurence said, echoing her, when Reed had opened the door to him. "I've never set foot in this place."

"It's not that you weren't welcome at any time," Kate said. "But we don't give parties, you and I don't meet that often, and when we do it's usually under your auspices."

"I see," Laurence said. He evidently had more immediate issues on his mind. "I've been pushing

169

contacts, calling in chips, making demands, you know, on behalf of your . . . finding out about Jay. And I'll tell you what I have decided; I don't believe he was ever in the Witness Protection Program."

Kate stared at her brother. "What do you mean? Do you think he's lied about the whole thing?"

"Not exactly. I think he did go into hiding; he did change his name to whatever it is—Smith or something. He did marry a woman under that name. Maybe he was hiding out, but not under the Witness Protection Program. I knew the guy was a phony the minute I laid eyes on him."

This was hardly true, but Kate decided not to make a point of it. She turned toward Reed, who was nodding.

"What are *you* nodding about?" she asked him. For reasons she could not have explained, she felt suddenly irritable and annoyed with both men.

"I'm not exactly surprised you think that," Reed said. "But I suspect it's because not even your influence could penetrate the secrets of the Witness Protection Program. Please don't take it personally," he added as Laurence looked offended. He gestured toward Laurence, trying to calm him. "I've been working on the other end, trying to discover if he ever stole a painting, or helped to steal one, and if he ever testified against someone who was convicted of murder."

Kate rose to her feet about to explode with anger.

"I didn't mention it," he said to Kate, "because I couldn't learn anything conclusive, and I didn't want you to have to confront suspicions that were without foundations. I thought it was enough discovering your father at this time of life."

"I see," Kate said, scarcely containing her anger. "Since I was coping with this familial shock, I couldn't be allowed to face up to anything else?"

"That's not exactly right."

"I see. And are we to be honored with a clear explanation, or have you undertaken this investigation purely as a solo performance?"

Laurence looked from one of them to the other as though he had suddenly found himself in a different place than he had supposed. "Kate, my dear," he began, but Reed held out a silencing hand.

"I can't hope to convince you of my motives," Reed said to Kate, "but I can at least explain them. I could not be certain, I simply could not be certain that my reasons for these investigations were more than irrational fears, petty resentments, and a rather terrifying sense of being out of control. I don't know whether I was more fearful of upsetting you for no reason, or worse, for my own shameful reasons, or having all my suspicions disproved and looking a fool and nasty into the bargain. I don't think my decision not to tell you what I was up to was a wise or defensible one, and I was going to tell you all about it just when Laurence arrived."

A sarcastic remark, doubting this, rose to Kate's lips, but she repressed it; she had never felt this violently angry with Reed before, and some sense of caution came to her aid.

"I've behaved like an idiot," Reed said. "And the worst part of it is I don't really know why. But it wasn't to betray you or go behind your back, however it looks."

Laurence waited out a short silence, and then asked if they might get back to talking about Jay.

171

"He's obviously a liar; he could have lied about most of his story. Were you able to find out anything?" he asked Reed.

"Only negatively. My investigator couldn't find evidence of a minor robbery in a small museum in San Francisco nearly fifty years ago. That doesn't prove much. I did discover that the number of paintings that have been done on Shakespearean subjects is vast; vaster than vast. The chance of finding if a particular subject had been painted, and when, and by whom, is negligible, at least for anyone provided with less than a year off and a small fortune."

"And the murder and the witness and all that?" Laurence asked before Kate could say anything, not that she appeared ready to speak.

"Negative again. The guys I know at the FBI, now or before, are willing to tell me a certain amount. But when it comes to paroled killers, there are, I regret to say, far too many of them to sort through; parole boards work in waves, and there are other influences on the question of pardons. In short, I have nothing substantive to report."

"How about less-than-substantive?" Kate asked, knowing her man, at least in this regard, and the exactness of his words.

Reed nodded at her. "Right you are," he said. "I've talked to him a good bit in the last few days . . ."

At this, Laurence started to rise to his feet, ready to demand an explanation.

"We'll explain it later," Kate said. "He was here; he's not here any longer; he's not here now," she repeated since Laurence seemed about to have a fit.

"Go on," she said to Reed. Laurence subsided, his mouth still open.

"Conversing with Jay," Reed went on, "getting a sense of him, I came to the conclusion that whatever the truth of his stories, two assertions of his were undeniable: that he had loved Kate's mother—and yours, of course, Laurence—and that he would not willingly have put Kate in danger. That does not mean that he may not have put her in danger without intending to, but I am certain he would not intentionally expose her to peril or risk her life. Therefore, he was either pretending to hide out in order to be near her, or he had got himself and her into an unforeseeable trap. What I did manage to do was to get him out of here without danger to himself if he was in danger, and thus without danger to Kate. Actually, I had come to believe that his stories were fabricated, that he wasn't in danger, but that I couldn't, yet, confront him with this. I needed proof."

Reed told Laurence of the plans he had made for Jay, and that these plans had been successfully carried out.

"You seem to have a certain amount of influence yourself," Laurence said, his tone a mixture of admiration and disbelief.

"Only in my world of crime. Big money goes further. I mean no offense," he added.

"None taken," Laurence said. "Money had better go far; it's what keeps the wheels turning."

It was evidence of Kate's unhappiness—guilt toward Reed, and worry about Jay—that she didn't answer Laurence even with a quip.

"The damn thing is," Laurence said, "and I came

173

here intending to tell you this although I didn't know you had actually been harboring that man, that I was responsible for some men trying to get in here to see if you were, in fact, harboring him. They couldn't get in but they became convinced you weren't. If they were mistaken, I'd like to know."

"They weren't mistaken," Reed said. "He wasn't here then."

"Well, I'm relieved to hear that," Laurence said. "I'll be off then. Will you let me know if you discover anything else about Kate's, er, father?"

"Yes," Reed said. "And may we expect the same from you?"

"Did you in fact come here because you expected to find him here?" Kate asked Laurence as he prepared to depart.

"I have my reports," he said, rather hastily. "Glad to know I was wrongly informed."

"At least you got to see where I live," Kate said, not graciously.

"Rather shabby," Laurence said. "Just what I expected. I know you could afford to hire a good decorator. Why not ask Janice to recommend one?"

Vastly to Kate's credit, she did not answer him; his manners seemed to her beyond sarcasm, as she later explained to Reed.

They had, of course, a great deal to explain to one another, and happily Laurence went and left them to it.

It was . . . an excellent play,
well digested
in the scenes, set down with as
much modesty as cunning.

Seventeen

THE FOLLOWING AFTERNOON Reed called Ringley at the police precinct to check on Jay's arrival at the upstate prison facility.

"He's not there, of course," Ringley said. "We handed him over to your men; they took him away."

"What do you mean, my men?"

"They had a note from you, and identification as agents with the Witness Protection Program. They looked official as hell. And your man didn't make any fuss about going with them. They got in a car and drove off."

"I don't suppose they said where they were going?" Reed asked, controlling his anger and frustration.

"They said they'd be in touch with you when they got there. They said: 'tell Amhearst we'll let him know as soon as we arrive.' "

"Arrive where?"

"They didn't say. They seemed to think you knew; I assumed you did. Is something wrong?"

"Never mind, Ringley," Reed said. "Thanks for all you've done."

Reed, who was in his office, phoned home; the message machine told him Kate had not yet arrived there. She was usually home by four on Wednesday afternoons unless she had told him otherwise, which she hadn't. He left a message for her to wait for him at home; he would be right there.

He had given the police both of his phone numbers. He presumed, however, that the agents, if they called at all, would call him at home. He rushed from the building that housed his office, stopping only to lock his office door. He sped down the stairs, out into the street, hailed a taxi—it was, thank God, the hour when taxis were heading downtown for the end of their shift—and arrived home, there to await Kate's return.

"You don't suppose they were agents from the Witness Protection Program?" Kate had asked when she arrived home and learned Reed's news.

"Of course not. They don't go trailing after people who have left the program, and certainly they wouldn't have known or cared where Jay was. But it does indicate that whoever this man is who's pursuing Jay, and whoever his accomplice is, they're smooth, they can look federal enough to fool a police officer, and they must have faked their identification badges skillfully. This man is not your ordinary roughneck or criminal; I'd say he's definitely middle-class and educated, or giving a damn good imitation. No, I'm not being snobbish or classist, I'm being a detective."

Kate had not yet thought of an answer to this when the telephone rang. Reed picked it up, saying "Amhearst" into the phone, as though he were still in his office. He never answered their home phone that way. Although he had spoken with some calmness to Kate, this was a sign of his anxiety. He did not speak again; he listened. Finally he said: "I'll have to call you back. No, I can't say anything before I speak to her. I won't speak to anyone else. Give me a number where I can reach you." Reed jotted a number down and hung up the phone.

"What?" Kate said.

"He wants you to meet him. You alone. They've got Jay. They say if you don't meet now, as soon as you can get there, they'll kill him. I said I had to talk to you. They gave me a number."

"And if you gave it to the police, could they rescue Jay?"

"Obviously not. It must be the number of the phone where they are, and they're going to have to tell you or me that anyway if they expect you to show up there. Probably it's the number of a public phone box near where they are. The police would never get there in time; this guy knows what he's doing."

"What is he doing?"

"I mean he's a clever operator. Of course you can't go, Kate. The question is, what are we going to do?"

"Do you think he'll kill Jay if I don't show up?"

Reed would later say that her question forced him to the hardest decision of his life. If he said no, they won't kill him, he would have lied to her; when she learned that he had lied, something between them would have been destroyed, perhaps irremediably. If he said what he believed, that they would kill Jay if Kate did not appear, she would probably insist on going; well, at least she would know the facts and be able to make her own decision. With all they had been through since this man, Jay, had entered their lives, his and Kate's alliance, their love, their marriage, had been tested, had been stretched further than ever before. If he lied to her, he might lose her. If he didn't lie, he might lose her anyway; she might be killed. With all that rushing through his mind, he never really doubted that the decision must be hers, and that she must decide on the basis of what he believed to be the truth.

"Yes," he said, "I'm afraid Jay will be killed if you do not go. That seems this man's supreme aim in life, if we are at all to trust what Jay has told us, and to judge from the man's voice on the phone, and from his actions, we can hardly mistrust his stated intentions."

They sat in silence for a period, probably short; minutes pass slowly under such circumstances; time is not fixed. Kate, tasting the silence, thought of Faustus's plea: go slowly, slowly, horses of the night.

"Faustus didn't know from slowly," she said to Reed.

"What?"

"I was thinking about time. Call the man, Reed; tell him I'll come. I have to, surely you see that. It was probably inevitable from the moment Jay entered Laurence's office that something like this would happen. Or is that only hindsight? Call him back. And write out clear directions; I'd hate to get lost."

Reed did not respond at once. He waited for what seemed to Kate another longish period. He wanted to speak to Kate, to say something, that was clear enough, but in the end he didn't speak. He dialed the number given; Kate could tell that the phone was answered immediately.

"She'll come," Reed said. "Yes, she has a car. She needs directions. She'll be alone; she won't be followed. But listen, I know her, she's a good driver but a lousy navigator. If she's late, it will be because she's lost. Don't panic. She is coming and she will be alone. Yes, she's leaving now. She has to get the car from the garage; it's two blocks away. Please, don't panic. Please be reasonably patient."

Kate turned west from the garage and then onto the Henry Hudson Parkway. Waiting on the street for the light to change, she had studied Reed's directions yet again; she had read them over and over in the garage while they were bringing her car down in the elevator. She had seemed, she was, impatient, and the garage man grumbled that he hadn't had any notice, he was getting the car as fast as he could.

Kate was to go from the Henry Hudson Parkway on to the Sawmill River Parkway, then turn off it quite soon. She had been told to take the right-hand road at the exit, and then the first right-hand turn she came to. She would then come almost immediately to a row of abandoned, boarded-up stores. They would be in the first one she came to, the man had said to Reed. She was to drive past the stores, leave the car farther up the road, and walk back to the store. She and her car would be watched; they would know if she was not alone.

179

To Kate's immense relief, the turnoff was easily found, as was the right-hand turn after that, as were the abandoned stores. The first one, toward which she was to walk after parking the car, seemed to have been some sort of ice cream place. Farther up the road—she had no idea how far was meant—she stopped the car; after some thought, she decided not to lock it. True, it might be stolen, but suppose she wanted to get away fast. She vaguely perceived that this decision made little sense, but she stuck by it all the same.

Approaching the boarded-up ice cream parlor, she looked for a door. A man standing at the corner of the building beckoned to her, indicating that she was to walk toward him. She followed him around to the back of the building and through an open door. The room she entered was dark; coming from the bright sunlight, she was for a moment blinded, unable to make out anything at all. During that moment of waiting for her eyes to adjust, she found herself to be, in the odd way (as she later surmised) of deeply introspective people, simultaneously frightened and thinking of how she would describe her fright. It was almost as though her fear were packed down inside her, not making itself evident to her mind or body, just unmistakably there. It was a new experience and gave her a sense of power, even as she knew herself to be, somewhere deep within her, terrified. Perhaps that was how it was with men in battle?

Gradually, her vision returned. There were three men in the room, each seated oddly on a tall stool, probably left over from the ice cream parlor. Jay was one of the men, just sitting there, not shackled in any way, indicating with ominous clarity that he was constrained by the other men, both of whom held guns; only one of the men sat with his gun pointed at Jay. The other man, his gun held in his hand, his hand resting in his lap, was the person in charge. Kate would be asked later why that was so immediately clear. The answer was a class answer: The man in charge was not a hired hand, or a thug, but rather a man like Jay: college educated, urbane of speech, with an air of natural authority. Also, it had been the other man, the man now pointing his gun at Jay, who had waited for Kate and beckoned to her to go around to the back of the building. He was a different sort from Jay and his pursuer, the product of a different world. Kate felt apologetic about this explanation, but there it was.

"Sit down," the man in charge said. "My name is Charles, not that it matters. I've never been called Charlie."

He pointed to another high stool, across the room from him and Jay, next to his partner with his gun at the ready. Kate clambered up onto the stool and sat, facing the two men. Suddenly she realized, though she could never understand why it had not occurred to her before, that Charles might shoot Jay, or tell the other man to shoot Jay, right before her eyes. Kate might not be able to imagine the man's reasons for shooting Jay in front of her, but whatever the reasons, they were doubtless a symptom of obsession. The man noticed the look of horror on her face, and reassured her.

"I'm not going to shoot him, not right now," he said. "Had I wanted to shoot him, I didn't need to send for you. Shooting a man before his daughter's eyes is not my immediate aim. It may never be my aim; it all depends on how you conduct yourself."

Kate, having somewhat recovered herself ("Did you know you can actually feel the blood come back into your head?" she would ask Reed later), looked directly at Jay. Jay tried to smile at her, but his demeanor suggested someone experiencing a profound indifference toward everything.

"He believes me that I will not injure you," the man said, as though he could read Kate's thoughts. Well, apparently he could read her thoughts, which under the circumstances was hardly the work of genius. "You're here to listen. His punishment, whether or not I kill him after you have left, will be to listen as you hear what this noble man, your father, has been up to for most of his life. Are you ready?"

All I could think of, Kate said later, was the children's game of hide-and-seek: Ready or not, I'm coming. It was clear my readiness was not an issue. Kate nodded all the same, and squirmed a bit on her stool trying to get more—well, comfortable was hardly the word, but less cramped. The man sitting near her raised his gun, positioning himself into greater alertness, but she soon settled down.

"And what has your newfound father told you about our long relationship?" Charles asked.

There was a long pause as Kate searched for words.

"Never mind," Charles said. "I'll tell you what he has admitted to you about his past: that he took part in an 'honorable' burglary, that I was there, that later he learned I had killed a man during another burglary, that he testified against me and was therefore responsible for getting me convicted. Is that about it?"

Kate nodded.

"Speak up. We're recording this, the way they do in the police station. You have to speak up so that the machine can hear you."

"Yes," Kate said. "That's what he told me."

"He suggested I was a cold-blooded killer, carried a gun"—here he waved his gun in the air—"and should have been put away for life."

"Not exactly," Kate said.

"But, put a bit more delicately, that was the idea, wasn't it?"

Kate nodded, then caught herself. "Sorry," she said. "Yes, that was the idea."

"Good; at least we've got that bit behind us. Would you like to go to the bathroom? I know fright does make one have to go. We haven't got a proper ladies' room, but please make use of what we have if you need to."

Kate did need to. She had been worrying about whether she could ask, and where she could go if she did ask and Charles said yes. "I'd like to go to the bathroom," she said.

"Fred here will show you where it is. He'll wait outside the door, but you'll be private. We don't mind waiting, do we, Jay?"

Fred got off his stool and gestured with his gun for Kate to get off hers. She followed him through a door she hadn't noticed and down a short hall to a small dirty room with a toilet and sink. "Would you like to make use of the facilities?" a pompous man had once asked her. Why should she remember that now? But at least Charles spoke direct, clear English, neither euphemisms nor that slang now current with the educated classes. Why on earth should she find that hopeful? Did that indicate that he was likely to be more reasonable or less? Villains in literature were often polite.

When Kate and her escort returned to the room, she was offered a glass of water, which she welcomed. Fright induces thirst.

"Good," Charles said. "Now, shall I begin?"

He seemed actually to be waiting for a signal from her to continue. Kate nodded, then immediately said, "Yes, please begin."

We might have been in a play by Sartre or someone, she said later to Reed. I suspected and feared that he was lulling me into acquiescence, even into admiration for him, or at least a willingness to hear him out. At the same time, I wanted to hear what he would say. At the back of my mind, as Jay sat on his stool, allowing his head to droop with tiredness, I feared for him. My God, I said to myself, he's over seventy years old.

And then it occurred to me, she told Reed, that Charles was also seventy or a bit more. He was the same age as Jay.

Charles began to speak, slowly, taking his time, as though he had been planning for a long time what he would say if he ever got the right chance to say it.

How say you?
My prisoner or my guest? by
your dread
"verily" one of them you
shall be.

Eighteen

"**J**AY AND I were at college together. We were roommates. He was best man at my wedding. That's where he met your mother. So far, that's what he told you, yes?"

This time he didn't wait even for a nod but went right on. He was talking to Kate, but he was talking for Jay; he was telling Jay his version, he was making Jay listen to Kate listening to his, Charles', version. That was his pleasure. Kate could only hope it would complete his pleasure, that shooting or other violence would not be required; that talking would suffice.

"So Jay met your mother at my wedding," Charles continued, "and it was instant love, across a crowded room, fireworks—in short, passion. My guess is that Jay met an older woman who wanted his love rather than alcohol, and your mother, if you'll forgive my mentioning it, hadn't been made proper love to and was smart enough to know it and to want it. Or

185

maybe she was enchanted, too, and just wanted the experience of a younger man; who knows? Anyway, lo and behold, you appeared a year or so later. And after that, your mother does not wish to run off with Jay here; in fact, she wants him out of her life, particularly since no one's noticed that this baby girl doesn't exactly resemble the other Fanslers. But then, she's a girl, which nicely explains everything. As for your mother, passion is one thing; practicalities quite another. Jay felt like shit, and I for one don't blame him. Not," he paused, as though Kate had interrupted him, "not that I blame your mother either. But it did complicate matters between Jay and me. To put it mildly. In fact, it screwed things up in a really big way."

Kate glanced to her right to see how the second man, gun still at the ready, was taking all this. Evidently he wasn't paid to listen, just to be present and on the alert with his gun. He probably thought all this nonstop talking was for types like Charles and Jay, who couldn't do much else in the way of action, and had to hire types like him for backup. That, at least, was what Kate was pretty sure Fred was thinking.

"Don't worry about Fred," Charles said, as though he could read her thoughts, and not for the first time, Kate noticed. Am I that obvious, she wondered, or is this an easy situation to read? The latter, I think.

"What had it to do with me, Charles? you are asking yourself. What did I care about whether or not Jay hung around on the outskirts of the Fansler world? Good question." Kate in fact had not thought of that question; her cognitive processes had defi-

186

nitely slowed down. She seemed to stay on the right side of fear, even hysteria, by thinking only on a rather superficial, partially attentive level; she knew herself to be incapable of complex or cogent thought.

"Well, as Jay's daughter and as a Fansler yourself—and keeping that name rather than taking your husband's made it much easier to find you, for which many thanks—as a Fansler you will, I know, be shocked to learn that I am an art thief and was, even then, though very few people knew that; not even the wife I was married to at the time had a clue; we've since gone our separate ways. Would you like another glass of water? Fred here will get it for you."

Kate said she would appreciate more water. Fred, whose head had come up at his name, rather as Banny's did, Kate thought, went off to get the water. Kate drank most of it when the glass was handed to her.

"This may get even thirstier," Charles said. "Sorry I can't offer you a more interesting drink. Your father doesn't drink, as you may know. I guess that's why he wanted a mother-figure like your mother, a woman who was a lady and didn't drink. Where was I?" But of course he remembered exactly where he had got to.

"I'd been Jay's roommate; I'd been his friend. He was my best man. But the truth of the matter, dear Ms. Fansler, is that it wasn't until Jay was in your mother's bed and out of his mind with amorousness that I told the poor chap what I wanted from him. You were on the way by then, which put even more power into my hands. Are you taking all this in?"

Kate nodded, and then proclaimed that she was

indeed listening most carefully, which, she later said to Reed, was the most absolutely inexact statement she had ever uttered. The best she could manage at the time, she told Reed, was to catch the drift.

"Right," Charles continued. "Well, not to beat about the bush, I was by the time of my wedding not only an art thief, I was a very accomplished practitioner in that calling, top of the field you might say. And there was Jay all lost to passion with Madame Fansler, who moved in the richest of circles, amid a most efficient and happy group of art collectors. Do you begin to get the idea?"

"Not exactly," Kate said, which was the simple truth.

"And here I thought you were a clever girl, a professor and all. Well, if needs must, I'll draw you a clearer picture. Are you concentrating?"

Kate nodded. She felt a slight urge to defend herself by pointing out that to be sitting on a stool, surrounded by two strange men with guns as well as one's newly discovered father was not a situation exactly conducive to clear, perceptive thinking. But to say that required more energy than she wished to expend at that moment, so she just said "Do go on."

"What I wanted of Jay and your mother was some guidance to their world of the rich, especially those who bought art and kept it at home on their walls to pretend they knew how to judge art. Of course, what they knew how to judge was the dealers who found the art for them, and those dealers knew what was hot and what would become even hotter. Sometimes, though not often, these rich friends of the Fanslers got a chance to buy something old and valuable and just a teeny bit foggy as to its provenance. I wanted to know where the art was, what the situation was, and then I wanted to steal it. I didn't put it that way exactly to Jay; not at first. I said that I could sell the information, which would earn me credit in my professional circles. I didn't mention right away that I planned to steal the pictures myself."

"I'm following you," Kate said, since he seemed to want some indication of her attention. If he expected her to become upset by what she was hearing, he would have to be patient. Given the chance, she would have liked to suggest that conversations taking place under pleasanter, less constrained circumstances were likelier to evoke more satisfactory responses. In truth, Charles was certainly getting more and more of her astonished concern as his story proceeded, but she considered it wiser not to reveal this.

"Well, dear Kate, your papa was not very quick about getting his newfound love, your mother-to-be, to cough up the information I wanted. I was getting slightly impatient, as you may imagine, but I didn't want to put on too much pressure and perhaps ruin the whole plan. And then, just as I was about to tell Jay that I would go to Mr. Fansler and reveal the whole affair between his wife and Jay, you were born. And within a very short time, or so it seemed to me, Jay had been handed his hat and told to get lost, though doubtless this was hedged in more delicate language with many explanations and persuasions being offered. The upshot was that Jay took off. He left full of anger, resentment, despair and a wish to put himself as far away as possible from his lost lady love—i.e., your mother."

"Go on," Kate said.

"Ah, encouragement," Charles said. "I may safely assume that you are indeed heeding my words."

"Yes," Kate said. "I am."

"Good. I got hold of Jay just before he cleared out and told him either he went to his lady love for the information I wanted, and convinced her to continue providing that information, or I would go to her, threatening of course to tell her husband about all the hanky-panky in his very own house with his very own wife. Jay was, as you might expect, furious and refused my request in an exceedingly rude fashion. To say he was insulting hardly represents his words or manner."

Kate glanced over at Jay. "In short," she said to Charles, "he told you to publish and be damned, the only possible words in which to answer a blackmailer."

"We are waking up, I see. Well, you are right. He said if his affair had to come out, then let it, though I knew he didn't mean that for a moment. He was bluffing, of course. He said he wasn't going to play any part in thieving and he doubted Louise, your mother, would either. Would you like another glass of water? I wouldn't mind having one myself. Do you think you could find another glass, Fred?"

Fred departed presumably to look for another glass. He returned to say he couldn't see any other glass, and they were damn lucky to have that one which someone must have left by mistake. He proffered the one glass now filled with water to Charles.

"No," Charles said. "Offer it first to the lady. Drink all you want, my dear. Fred can always fill it

190

again." But Kate, not wishing to aggravate Fred, drank only half of the water in the glass and then handed the glass to Fred to hand to Charles. Not much action in this play, she thought. Even Beckett had more action than this, not to mention better dialogue or monologue as the case might be.

"So there was our Jay, taking off in a cloud of dust and despair, and I was left to consider what my next move might be. After a time, I decided to visit the lady herself—your mother, my dear. Getting to see her was no great problem; we had met at my wedding and she knew me to be a friend of Jay's. Perhaps she even wanted to see someone who reminded her of Jay, brought him to mind so to speak. Her complete innocence and pleasure at the thought of seeing me demonstrated clearly enough that Jay had told her nothing of my plan, or indeed anything about me, let alone that I was a purloiner of art. I didn't mention my nefarious scheme at our first little chat—she served me tea, and let me google at you in your cradle. But at my second visit, some weeks later—it never pays to rush this sort of thing—I confessed the truth of my profession, as I called it; she was shocked, but a smart lady, no doubt of that. Her first question was, did Jay know? You still with me, dear?"

Kate assured him that she was, paying heed to every word she might have added, but didn't.

"Here I made an important and, as I came to think, clever decision. I told her that Jay knew nothing of this, that unlike me he was boringly straight and honorable, as I was not. In fact, I added, I had hoped that she might be willing to help me in my less-than-honest endeavors. Doing so, I pointed out, might add a certain element of adventure and danger to her rather overmeticulous and mundane life. I was in high hopes this idea would appeal to her, and had she shown the slightest inclination to consider that challenge, I would have left her to ponder it and, I might have hoped, to persuade herself to add this touch of spice to her daily round. But no such luck. She flatly refused even to contemplate so dishonest a scheme, and ordered me to depart, in the most formal and ladylike if unmistakable manner. You, no doubt, would have responded in the same way: stiff, dismissive, but not obviously rude."

"Perhaps," Kate said. I would certainly like to say something exceedingly rude at this very moment, Kate thought, but did not utter the words. After all, her mother had not had a gun pointed at her at that particular moment, to say nothing of the other men present.

"Even with so definite a refusal," Charles continued, "I decided to leave it a while. The more certain upright types are of refusing to be dishonest or illegal, the more attractive the opportunity to be just that often becomes upon reflection, when they've had time to convince themselves they wouldn't be doing anything really wrong. But not with your mama, as I discovered upon my return visit.

"Of course, she didn't want to see me, and told the servant to tell me she did not care to see me. I, however, had come prepared for this rejection, had asked the servant to return to her with a note I had written in advance for just such an eventuality. The note said—well, naturally I can't remember the exact wording but it conveyed that she would certainly find herself acutely unhappy if she continued in her refusal to allow me an audience with her. It was a nice, formal, threatening note.

"She let me come into her presence after that, and the odd thing is that I now suspect she thought it was Jay I was threatening to harm. But that didn't occur to me at the time. So I took a seat across from her—she was making some sort of tapestry thing, I remember, needle being pulled way out on a long thread, then pushed through to the other side and pulled out again—and I promised her that if she didn't agree to help me, I would go to her husband and offer him a similar bargain. In that case, of course, I would threaten to make public the fact that his daughter was not his. We didn't have DNA then, so I could not have proved it, but I was certain once the idea was in his head, he would find plenty of reason to believe me. You didn't exactly look like his other children, as you may have noticed."

Kate said that she had hardly in her youth paid much attention to any such dissimilarities between herself and her brothers, but certainly could both notice and remember the differences now.

"And what did my mother say in answer to that?" Kate asked. By now she was altogether attentive, not to say transfixed.

"Here's the funny part," Charles said, looking over at Jay. "She said that I should go right ahead and do whatever I had to do. She would play no role of any sort in any of it. Now that surprised me, so I went away and had a little think. And you know what I concluded, Jay old boy?" Charles turned toward Jay, who did not move. "Look at me when I talk to you," Charles said, raising his gun a slight bit. Jay sat upright then and looked at Charles.

"That's better," Charles said. "What I concluded was that, for the most part, your mother simply didn't believe I would do it, would go to Mr. Fansler and tell him all about his wife's hanky-panky, not to mention the fetching, hardly legitimate result now making a legitimate claim on his fortune and his sacred honor. Maybe that's what she figured. But you know what else I think she figured, Jay old boy? Maybe not consciously, not altogether consciously, but figured all the same: that if the truth about her love affair was revealed, that if she was thrown out into the cold without a cent and her daughter cast off with her, well, then she would have to find you, wouldn't she, Jay, and make a life with you after all? Maybe she hadn't been quite so certain about her decision to stay with Fansler; maybe she wanted to give fate one more chance to intervene. What do you think, Jay?"

Kate did not look at Jay; she did not want to see his face. Instead, she turned slightly more toward Charles and said, "Please go on. I can't sit on this stool forever, and I don't mind telling you that I may just get down off it and walk away. If you or Fred decides to shoot me, that's what you'll have to do. And then you can shoot Jay, too. I'm quite serious, so please, let's get to the end of this story."

Her only motive was to divert Charles' attention away from Jay. But even as she spoke these threatening words, it occurred to her that they were not entirely untruthful. She straightened her back and lifted her feet from the rungs of the stool; she moved them about, even stretched them out. In do-

194

ing so, she was reminded of sitting across from the cot in the maid's room with her feet stretched out between Jay and Reed. But she must not think of Reed; for some reason her lucidity and dignity depended on not thinking about Reed. "Do get on with it," she said again.

"The woman I had married also moved in the same circles as the Fanslers, which is why the Fanslers had been at my wedding. Maybe, I had thought, I could make my wife my partner in this scheme and not have to tackle Mr. Fansler. But it didn't take me long to realize that my wife, while she would no doubt be happy to take part in anything exciting, illegal, and dangerous, had all the self-discipline of a rutting ram. Ours, I'm afraid, was one of those alliances based on lust and the refusal to discover before marriage anything fundamental about our spouse-to-be. As I've said, we didn't stay together long.

"So it was back to Mr. Fansler I had to go. I went to see him in his office, probably the same sort of office where Jay went to call upon your brother Laurence. Oh, yes, I knew all Jay's movements; once I'd identified you I had no problem following our boy every step of the way. Back then, however, when I was approaching Mr. Fansler, I think the poor man probably thought I'd come to beg for a job, or, anyway, his help in finding one. Once I sat down and began talking, of course, he was sadly disabused of such a speculation. I told him what I wanted, and what the price was."

"You told him," Kate exclaimed. "You told him Jay was my father and all the rest of it?"

"Yes, I did, my dear. He went white, absolutely

white. I thought he was going to pass out, to tell you the truth, and I'd got out of my chair and moved over to him, but he waved me away. I poured him a glass of water—there was a carafe with glasses on a nearby table, it was that kind of office—but he just kept shaking his head. Then he said: 'Get out!' to me. He shouted it, and rose from his chair behind his desk. He swayed a minute, but held on to the desk, and then shouted again for me to get out and never come back. And then I understood."

"What?" Kate said, all pretense at indifference abandoned.

"I realized he thought I had told him about Jay just for the hell of it, for the fun of upsetting him and making trouble; I could see that's what he thought. 'You've got it wrong,' I said. 'I may be a crook; I am a crook, but I'm not a mean, slimy bastard. I told you about Jay and your wife and your supposed daughter because I want something in exchange for not telling the world.'

"Well, then he began to see. He called me a blackmailer and used every despicable name he could come up with, and then shouted at me again to get out.

" 'But what about my proposition?' I asked. 'Shall I tell the world, or will you do what I ask? It's not very difficult, and I won't ask for information very often. I don't want to risk my own reputation, never mind yours.' Of course, he didn't yet know what information I was after. Probably he thought something financial, insider-trading, that sort of thing. I didn't sense that he could take in much more, so I said I was leaving. I put my card down on his desk. 'Call me when you want to discuss this further,' I said. 'I won't do anything in the meantime, but don't keep me waiting too long.' And I left."

"So he knew," Kate said. "All along, he knew."

"Yes, my dear Kate, he knew almost from the beginning of your life. He certainly knew."

Your tale, sir, would cure deafness.

Nineteen

KATE WAS STUNNED for a moment into immobility. Then, as though she were somewhere else, as though she were altogether unaware of her surroundings, she leapt from the stool onto her feet to stand facing Jay.

"You might have told me that minor fact," she said. "With all your storytelling, all your accounts of never-diminishing passionate love, you might have included the fact that my father knew all along. Didn't it strike you that that was a rather, shall we say, *momentous* fact, something of significance?"

Before Jay answered her, if indeed he meant to answer her, Fred and Charles were on their feet and, one on each side, lifted her back onto her stool. Kate could not believe she was being manhandled, but the force of their hands on her arms woke her to the actuality of the situation. Fred had his gun out and was looking at Charles for orders. Charles, having loosened his grip on Kate, and having waved Fred back to his stool, looked at Kate for a long moment and asked: "May I continue?"

But Kate was not feeling as docile as she had been. "I don't know how long we've been here, attending to your monologue about your life adventures," she said, her tone dry, "but Reed is not going to sit home wondering what's become of me for many more hours, I can promise you that. And if that means that Fred here is going to shoot me, I'm not sure that wouldn't be preferable to perching on this stool listening to your narcissistic rendition."

"I understand that you're upset by my revelation about your father—that is, your Fansler father, but try to contain yourself in patience a little longer. We haven't been here as long as you suppose. And there isn't much more to tell. But I do insist that Jay here attend to every word."

"Did my Fansler father play your game then?" Kate asked. She hoped Charles thought this was asked to hurry him along, but in fact she found that she had an urgent need to know the answer.

"Yes, he did, being a sensible man who responded in a sensible way. After all, I wasn't asking him to set me up for regular thieving from his associates and friends. We'd never have got away with it. No, we decided to go after one or two real gems, the second after an interval of some years, needless to say."

"He arranged for you to steal the valuable paintings of his friends?" Kate wanted to be quite sure she had this straight, had the exact truth of the matter.

"Perhaps I better remind you how the system works, or worked then. It probably still does, in fact. You steal the painting, you keep it nice and safe, and then you offer to give it back for ransom. Ransom is usually ten percent of the market price, in that neighborhood anyway. So if a painting is worth ten million, it is returned for one million cash, no questions asked. Yes, you're right, it is kidnapping, but the victim doesn't suffer, and the owner of the painting suffers only in his pocketbook. Insurance companies are glad to get off at that price, and no one pursues the robber, let alone his informer. Nice and neat, isn't it? Of course, insurance rates go up so everyone suffers to that extent, but most of them can afford it or they wouldn't have bought the picture in the first place."

"I can't believe it," Kate said. But even as she spoke, she realized all that she had been willing to believe about Fansler business methods, about the ways in which the very wealthy acted and were treated in America. Why was helping Charles to steal pictures that he knew would be returned so different? The bigger question, after all, was why he had not told anyone about his daughter's parentage.

Charles was back to reading her thoughts. "I often wondered whether he told your mother he knew about Jay, but I finally determined that he had said nothing. Was it because he feared to be shamed in the eyes of the world, or because he loved her, in spite of it all, and was glad that she had remained in his home as his wife?"

Kate turned to Jay. She had become quite expert at shifting herself around on the stool. "Remember that movie you keep talking about, the one where the man says he will love the woman all his life?" she asked Jay. Jay did not respond. "Do you remember how the movie ended?"

When Jay did not answer her question, Charles waved his gun. "Answer the lady," he said, "or I'll let Fred here put a bullet in a not-fatal place. He's itching to shoot that gun, I do assure you. He's tired of sitting there doing nothing. Answer the lady nicely now."

"It ended at the railroad station," Jay said. "She went off on the train."

"That's how the lovers parted, not how the movie ended," Kate said.

"Might I know what movie we're talking about here?" Charles asked.

"*Brief Encounter,*" Kate said. "And the movie ends as it began, with the woman sitting at home with her husband; she is remembering the love affair from its beginning, in all its detail. The movie is a flashback. And at the end, her husband says to her, as though he had guessed where she had been, 'Thank you for coming back to me.' That's how the movie ended. Funny that you didn't remember that. Perhaps if you had remembered it you would have been less in a rage with Papa Fansler."

"May I get on with my tale? I'm beginning to feel like the ancient mariner," Charles said. Kate waved a hand to say: go on. Charles spoke.

"Where was I? Oh, yes. Well, before Papa Fansler and I had managed to kidnap our paintings, our friend Jay here was involved in stealing a painting. Maybe you've heard about that?" It was a question; Kate nodded in response.

"I thought so. What he probably didn't tell was that it was he who brought me in on the job. He and the guy whose picture it was couldn't have robbed a newspaper from a blind vendor. We pulled it off ex-

201

actly as planned. I frightened the two innocents by carrying a gun, but I didn't expect to use it; I was just making sure that I didn't run into trouble with no means of protecting myself. It all came off easy as could be, however, and that was that. Move up twenty years more or less. Can you do that Kate?"

"I'm with you," Kate said.

"I wish you had been. I was involved in a big heist at a museum, much bigger than anything I attempted before, and one of the guards decided to be a hero. That screwed the whole thing up. We didn't get the pictures, and the guard was shot and killed. Who by? I don't know, but it wasn't me. I know that for certain, because I didn't fire my gun. The police took us all in, the museum got involved, the insurance company got involved, the security people got involved. There was a lot of publicity and outcry, and someone had to take the fall. It probably would have been one of my associates—a trigger-happy fellow like Fred here—except that our friend Jay offered to testify that he knew me to have a gun, to have committed art theft, and to be a likely suspect. He was a respected young architect, the best of witnesses. They believed him. They also promised to put him in the Witness Protection Program, even though I would be in jail, having been given a twenty-five to life sentence. It's always supposed that the convicted felon may have associates on the outside who will take revenge on the man who testified against their comrade. That's likelier with the Mafia and such, but it happens. Why did our Jay want to hide out, change his name, his place to live, all of it? Maybe he wanted a new life; maybe he wanted to punish himself for having been such a naughty boy with your mother. Your guess is as good as mine. You can imagine the rest. I said if I ever got out I would find him and kill him. I didn't know he would make it so easy by quitting Witness Protection and doing the one thing that would assure my catching up with him—that is, of course, going to look for you."

"But what can you gain by killing him now?" Kate asked. "Or by killing me, too? Reed knows about this rendezvous; you've won really. You've found us both. You've made us sit on stools and listen to you and grow thirsty and damned cramped and uncomfortable. Why not just let us go? I'll give you my word not to pursue you, which you probably won't believe, but what could I accuse you of if I did go after you, which I promise not to do? I doubt that anyone would believe the story of what went on in this abandoned ice cream parlor."

"Yatter away," Charles said. "I'll tell you what I'm going to do. I'm not going to kill Jay. At our time of life, what's the point? I want to stagger out of here free, just as you suggest, and I do believe you that you won't go after me or persuade your husband to go after me, or your brothers either. I don't think they know that your father knew, by the way, in case you were wondering."

"I was," Kate said.

"No. He had to keep it altogether to himself. No one was to know but him, me, and Jay, and Jay wasn't to know that Fansler knew, but that I couldn't agree with. I told him I was going to tell Jay, but that no one else would ever know—and until this moment, I have kept my word."

"Is that why Jay testified against you?" Kate

203

asked. "Because you told my Fansler father the truth."

"Got it in one," Charles said. "You are smart, I'll agree to that any day. I'm sure you'd have been just as smart with your Fansler father's genes, but in a different way. Maybe you'd have cornered the market instead of lecturing about literature. Yes, Jay was crazy with anger when I told him I'd told Fansler who the father of his daughter was. I don't know why it infuriated him so powerfully. I suspect that Fansler's knowing made it a dirty secret instead of a beautiful romantic secret, but maybe I'm getting literary from talking to you so long."

There was a long silence. Kate studied Jay, the new, strange father she had found subtly attractive, the man whose appearance had been so exhilarating and troubling an event. What did she think of him now? That he was a man who had got stuck in a long-ago passion—like a fly in amber, Kate thought. Not an original analogy, God knew, but a fitting one. And finally he had left his hiding place, gone back to his profession, which he was good at, one had to grant him that, and gone in search of the only living evidence of his great love. But I won't consent to be romantic evidence, Kate thought. I don't want to serve as his redemption for having given false testimony. I think we had better part as though we had never met in Laurence's club in the first place.

"Are you going to share your literary thoughts?" Charles asked.

"Yes, I am," Kate said. "May I offer you this solution for your need of revenge; can I persuade you that it is as cruel and satisfactory as killing Jay would be?"

"Let's hear it."

"If this will satisfy you, I will promise never again to see, talk to, meet with, or in any way correspond with Jay. He will be out of my life and I altogether out of his. You have kidnapped his daughter instead of a painting. You've brought it off and driven Jay and me apart again; that is your ransom. Let that be enough revenge. Let Jay and me go, separately. You can drop him off wherever you like. Knowing how I feel, he will not try to get in touch with me again. I will walk out to my car, drive off, and that will be the end of it. I will tell no one but Reed what has happened; Reed, I can give you his word and mine, will tell no one. Is it a bargain?"

"Nicely put. And I even believe you. I'm even willing to let you convince me that Reed will take no action, and that you will pick up your life exactly as it was before Jay entered it some short time ago. But it doesn't satisfy me. Sorry. I've had too many years to brood on this."

Charles looked at Fred, who nodded and went outside, perhaps to keep watch, perhaps for some reason Kate could not understand. "I'm not going to kill Jay. You're right about that. I've thought of something more suitable, some way to even things up between us. Did you notice that I limp?"

"No," Kate said. "I've hardly seen you walk. Do you limp?"

Charles slid off his stool and paraded up and down in front of Kate. One leg dragged somewhat behind the other; it had to be raised with a special effort and then put down again. Charles had got rather good at this, so that he did not lurch as much as, Kate supposed, he had shortly after the injury.

"I see," she said. "How did it happen?"

"In prison. Things like this happen in prison. I've had operations; I'm to have another. It's easier with a cane, but I left it at home today."

Kate knew what he was going to do. "Don't," she said. "It will serve no one; it will hardly satisfy you; it is evil; it will only do harm." But she could tell he wasn't listening.

"You go," he said to Kate. "Walk out the door, wave to Fred, get into your car, and drive off. You can tell Reed what has happened, but I have your word it will go no further. Even it if does, of course, you can do nothing. Jay won't talk, and there is no evidence. Fred and I will be certain there is no sign here of our presence, even if you should lead someone to this place. But I'm sure you won't. I'm glad to have known you, Kate."

He looked at her. He seemed to think of offering his hand, and decided against it. "Don't blame yourself for anything. You have saved your father's life, if not the intactness of his body. Always remember that. And do go and find him again one day soon. He needs you. He's an old man, like me, though neither of us looks it. If I had a daughter, I would want to know her in my last years. Go."

Kate hesitated. Sometimes it is possible to know exactly what can be done and what cannot be done. And yet, down from the stool, standing, she spoke once more. "As you know," she said, looking straight at Charles, "I profess literature." She paused, giving him time to tell her to shut up and go. He, too, paused and said nothing. Kate spoke.

"There is a sonnet of Shakespeare's—no, I won't offer you the whole sonnet, I don't even remember more than the first two lines: 'They that have power to hurt and will do none,/They do not do the thing they most do show.' One can never know exactly what Shakespeare meant, but certainly he understands that revenge is a powerful emotion, but that once the power to take revenge is definitely yours, the proof of that power is that you no longer need to hurt. Which is the best revenge."

She turned and went out. Fred stood outside and watched her walk up to her car. She did not turn to look back. Reed will never believe that I quoted Shakespeare, she thought. Who would believe it? But perhaps Reed would, after all, understand how words that demand to be uttered fly into the mind— anyway, into Kate's mind.

So Jay was out of her life. She would never know if he was to be shot in the leg or not. It was over. Reaching the car, she sat for a moment before starting the engine. Then, slowly, she fastened her seat belt; slowly she turned the car around. As she drove onto the Sawmill River Parkway, as she planned what she would say to Reed, she recognized that already the drama in that abandoned ice cream parlor was taking on the quality of a dream.

Twenty

WHEN KATE REACHED home, walking slowly from the garage, moving instinctively, as she had driven, she neither chose to talk nor desired the drink Reed offered her. She sat on the couch, huddled into herself. Reed sat down beside her, pulled her against him and held her in his arms.

"Just tell me you're all right," he said. "You can shake your head yes or no."

But Kate was able to say that she was quite as well as ever. "Nothing violent happened," she said. "It was a lot of words. There were two men with guns, but there are so many guns on television that these seemed like ordinary props. I'm very tired." She said no more.

After a time, when she had again refused food or drink, he helped her into bed and, lying beside her, offered silent support. They were silent for what seemed to Reed like hours; then she fell asleep.

Later, when she woke up, leaping, it seemed to

her, from a dream, Reed woke with her. "How goes it?" he asked.

"I'm really okay," she said. "Nothing happened. Only talk, endlessly, from Charles. On and on he went."

Reed did not ask who Charles was. He assumed him to have been the man on the telephone, the man obsessed with Jay. Reed did not ask anything. When she was ready, she would tell him. But he found his mind fixed on the two guns she had mentioned. So there had been another man, as Reed suspected there would be, another man besides Jay. It took more discipline than Reed had ever remembered mustering not to ask questions. He knew he must wait; it was necessary for her to speak, of course, therapeutically and practically. But he would wait.

"I'm hungry," Kate said.

"An omelet?"

"Lovely." They moved to the kitchen. "It's four o'clock in the morning," Kate said, looking at the kitchen clock. "Do you know what it's like?" she asked, as Reed got out the pan and butter and eggs. "It's like having been in an auto accident where only fenders were dented. Frightening, but no one was hurt, so why go on thinking about it? And yet, one remembers the moment of impact; one relives it."

She seemed suddenly to realize she was terribly thirsty. Going to the sink, she ran the water and drank many glasses of it, as though she had crossed a desert.

"Here's the omelet," he said.

But she ate only a bite or two before putting down her fork. "I might as well tell you," she said.

209

"Briefly. I'll fill in the empty spaces later. Is that all right?"

"Fine." He sat down beside her and took her hand; she smiled at him, a sad smile but he found it encouraging.

"We perched on stools; literally perched. Jay, and Charles, and me, and Fred. He was the other man with a gun. I felt he would have liked to use his gun, but he didn't. Charles talked. And talked and talked and talked. He said Jay had lied about his, Charles', part in the killing of a guard. He said a lot besides; I'll get to it eventually. This is what I want to tell now. Is that all right?"

Reed nodded. "Just what you want to tell," he said.

"Charles is an art thief; always has been. He tried to get Jay and my mother to direct him to works of art he might steal—works in the houses of the Fanslers' rich friends. Jay and my mother refused, so he went to my Fansler father. Here's the hard part." She paused, and Reed was not sure if she would go on. Neither, obviously, was she.

But she went on. "My Fansler father knew. About me and Jay and all. He knew almost from the beginning; Charles told him. Charles threatened to make the love affair public; he would keep quiet, he said, for leads to valuable paintings. So my Fansler father led Charles to a couple of very expensive pictures in exchange for Charles' silence. Do you understand, Reed? My Fansler father knew all along. And he never let on. He never said anything to my mother, or so it appears. He always accepted that I wasn't his daughter. And you remember what my brothers said about my right to inherit? He still left me my share of the money knowing I wasn't his daughter. He left me an equal share. In his way, I guess, he loved my mother as much as Jay did. Maybe more."

Reed pushed the plate with the omelet gently toward her, but she shook her head. "That's all there is," she said. "That's the main part of the story."

He guessed there was more. There had to be more. Threats to Jay if not to her. Threats to Jay that had to affect her. She would talk about it in good time; she had to talk about it, to him or to someone else; a therapist, perhaps, or her friend Leslie.

They sat quietly for a time. Reed gave her a glass of ice water, and she drank it. Then they went back to bed. Reed reached out to hold her, but she turned away, not unkindly, and seeming to want to lie by herself. He held himself awake until he could tell by her breathing that she was again asleep.

Kate went to work the next day. She took up her usual life and must have appeared quite normal to those she encountered during the day. To Reed she seemed to be grappling inside her head with recollections of her hours in the ice cream parlor, but she had told him little more of those hours beyond trying to convey the condition and the, well, atmosphere of the ice cream parlor. She described the stools they had sat on for so long. He asked only what Charles looked like, a question he thought inessential enough not be hectoring.

Kate looked puzzled for a moment. "He looked like Jay," she finally said. "Not exactly, of course. But they seemed the same height and the same shape and the same age. They were at college together," she added, as though that explained anything. Reed did not press the point. Kate had once mentioned to him that Queen Elizabeth the First had dealt with immediate threats by waiting, by letting time pass. Kate had apparently determined to follow that prescription.

As the days passed, Kate seemed to return to her usual self; she even began to chatter again, even quoted Shakespeare: " 'If this were played upon a stage now, I would condemn it as an improbable fiction,' " but she did not speak of that "improbable fiction" in any detail. The only references she made to her having been a prisoner in the deserted ice cream parlor were to more than once observe that there had been no violence, despite the guns. She sometimes repeated, without being asked, that nothing dramatic had happened. "Not while I was there," she would add, opening grounds for speculation as to what she feared had happened after she left, speculation that Reed restrained from giving voice to.

When some weeks had passed, and Reed feared that the memories of that time in the ice cream parlor had been repressed, or that their importance had been denied, Kate astonished him by announcing her intention to go down to Jay's apartment, the one they had visited, the one he still had the right to occupy. She thought she would look around; just to see if Jay was all right. She rather wanted to know if he was still living there.

"May I go with you?" Reed asked. He intended to accompany her with or without her consent, but he hoped for her consent.

"Why not?"

"We could, of course, telephone first."

"I thought of that. I'd rather go. He's either there or not. I don't know what I would find to say on the telephone."

Reed guessed that she wanted action, not talk. She wanted to do something, make some move. He would have felt the same. He had, in fact, been wondering about Jay and trying to decide if there were any steps he should take to discover Jay's condition, or his situation. On the other hand, Kate might never want to see Jay again, might not want Reed instigating any search, and that possibility had to be respected.

And so the next afternoon they set out to visit, if not Jay, Jay's apartment. It occurred to Reed that were Jay not there, and were they to request again to see the empty apartment, the superintendent might find this repeat visit more than a little suspicious and certainly peculiar. If Jay were not at home, Reed decided, they must either just depart or depart and leave him a note. At least they might learn from the doorman whether Jay had recently been seen on the premises. Reed feared, on Kate's behalf, that Jay might have moved out, left for some faraway, unknown destination. But Reed said nothing of this. She had probably thought of all the same alternatives he had been pondering; it was unnecessary to mention them now.

When they arrived at the apartment house, the door was guarded by a different man, one who had not been there at their former visit. They both smiled on greeting him, glad of that.

"Yes?" he said, in the manner of all such guardians of the gates. "Mr. Jason Smith," Kate said, omitting the Ebenezer. Suddenly she felt afraid. She did not know whether she was frightened of finding him there or of finding him gone.

"Your name?" the doorman asked. "Reed and Kate," Kate said. She had learned that it was better not to expect their surnames to be easily understood or repeated. Americans now lived in a first-name culture, and it was no use insisting on a formality that simply delayed whatever one was trying to accomplish.

The doorman called to Jay's apartment on the house phone. He rang for several minutes; he was just about to declare Mr. Smith out, when the house phone was answered.

"Reed and Kate are here," he said into the phone.

There was then a pause, while the doorman listened to the response. He turned to them when he had hung up the receiver and reported: "He says will you wait twenty minutes and then come up. He was asleep."

"Thank you," Kate said. There was a comfortable lobby, but Kate had noticed the last time they were there that Jay's windows looked out on a small garden, one probably reserved for tenants. She asked the doorman if they might sit there.

He hesitated, but evidently decided they were not of the vandalizing sort, and they were visiting a tenant who could have taken them down there if he had wanted to. He pointed to a door leading to the garden, and dismissed them.

The garden was pleasant, with benches and

gravel walks. They sat down on a bench. "I hardly know what to expect," Kate said.

"Or what to hope for?" Reed asked.

"I haven't a clue what to hope for. Except that he's in one piece."

"Why shouldn't he be? You said there was no violence, no gunshots."

"Not while I was there. I don't know what happened after I left. There were rumblings."

"Do you want to tell me about it before we ascend, so that I may have a clue what you two are talking about?"

"I've already told you the main facts; they're really all that I learned. But I'll repeat them." Kate paused, gathering her thoughts; then she rattled off the facts revealed during the session in the ice cream parlor, as though she were reciting a catechism: "Charles told my Fansler father about Jay being my father; Charles has always been an art thief, and blackmailed my Fansler father into leading him to a couple of valuable pictures; he stole them and received ransom, which was all he had intended to make on the deal. He claims that Jay lied in his testimony about the killing of the guard; he says he did not shoot the guard. That's about it," she added, after a moment's reflection; "I doubt you now know what to expect from Jay any more than I do."

She found she could not tell Reed that Charles had threatened to shoot Jay in the leg; to destroy his knee. She wanted to forget that, forget that such a thing could happen, forget that she cared so much that Jay might be injured. He had after all lied to them, told them made-up stories, put them in

215

danger. Why should she care if he was shot at, crippled? Well, she would care whoever it was, she told herself. And that was true. But she cared more than in that general way, and she hardly knew why.

They waited half an hour, to give Jay plenty of time to prepare for their entrance. Then, back in the lobby, they rang for the elevator, entered it, pressed the button for Jay's floor. Every action seemed weighted with meaning as, Kate thought, in one of those terribly arty, slow films where every frame was designed to have a powerful effect. But it was usually dark in those films, she thought. She wished her mind would settle down, to say nothing of her pulse, which was, at least to her ears, audibly racing. They left the elevator and rang Jay's bell.

Jay, when he opened the door, looked freshly showered. He had closed the door to the bedroom; as he ushered them into the living room Kate saw that he walked easily, with no impediment whatever. And what terrified her then was the realization that if she was ninety percent relieved, she was ten percent disappointed. Part of her wanted him to have suffered. Well, why not face it? Perhaps one needed to have been part of such a scene as that in the ice cream parlor really to know oneself.

Jay waved them to seats and asked if they wanted anything to drink: tea, water, Scotch—those were all he could offer—oh, and instant coffee. They said they were fine.

"Perhaps in a little while," Reed said, hoping to indicate this was not intended to be a short or quick visit.

Jay, too, sat down. "I'm not going to say I'm sorry for what you went through," he said to Kate.

"You must know how horrified I was by the whole thing. I could hardly have handled it worse, from the minute I knew he was after me."

"But he didn't kill you after all," Kate pointed out. "He didn't even shoot you," she added, glancing at his knees.

"It's something odd about long-planned revenge," Jay said. "When the chance finally comes to destroy the object of your long obsession, you don't do it. There are various reasons for this. One is that you don't want to take away the reason for your hatred. There may be a simple recognition that killing your enemy won't change anything in the past. There may be a sudden refusal to risk the possible consequences of murder or assault with a gun. I've been reading about it, up at the Columbia library. I got a pass to read there, but not to check out books."

"And which of these applied in your case?" Reed asked. "All of them, do you think—a bit of each?"

"Perhaps a bit of each," Jay said. "But the real cause of my escape was Kate; that she was there, that she heard Charles' story, that he saw, because of Kate's presence, that he had wounded me more seriously and more subtly than a gunshot would have done. And dead, I could hardly have suffered and I have suffered since, with regret, and self-damnation, and the knowledge that having found my daughter, I had lost her."

Kate felt herself unmoved by this speech; in fact, she felt further hardened against him, angry at being doled out plaudits rather than, well, rather than what? An admission of his idiocies? Perhaps he was right; perhaps her being there had saved him.

"I still wonder," she said to Jay, "why you lied

217

about Charles shooting that guard; why you testified against him knowing he hadn't shot the guard. Have you a tidy explanation for that?"

"Oh, yes," Jay said. "That's the easy part to answer. You see, I know he shot the guard because I saw him do it. I was there."

Kate looked stunned. "Why didn't Charles tell us that?"

Jay stood up. "Because no one was ever to know I had been there; I would have been charged as an accomplice. As it was, I just spoke of him in the past. Let me get you some tea. Then I'll tell you the whole story, nothing omitted, nothing untrue, no excuses."

"I'll help you get the tea," Reed said, rising.

The two men went into the kitchen, leaving Kate to walk to the window and stare out at the garden where they had waited for Jay to receive them, leaving Kate to some minutes' solitude, leaving her time to collect herself.

Twenty-one

WHEN REED AND Jay returned with the tea tray, Kate had regained her seat.

"Sorry; there aren't any cookies," Jay said.

"Let's not pretend this is a tea party," Kate said. "So you and Charles agreed to let you pretend you'd had no part in the robbery. Why didn't Charles tell me that during the scene in the ice cream parlor? It would have been an excellent piece of dialogue."

"He didn't tell you, and Charles didn't want me to tell the court at his trial, because he would have had no chance at an acquittal if it was known that I saw him shoot the guard, rather than that I knew him well enough to be certain he had shot the guard. As it turned out, he wasn't acquitted, but he might have drawn a stiffer sentence had my testimony been altogether honest."

"How did you happen to be there?" Kate had determined to keep the caustic quality out of her voice, but she had not wholly succeeded.

219

"May I start at the beginning?" Jay asked. "The whole story over again, but with a few more flourishes. Yes," he added, looking at Reed, "and a few more facts. No omissions, I promise. But I hope you will permit me some attempts at explanation. Not justification, I promise; just self-analysis."

They all sipped their tea. Jay began to speak while still seated, still holding his cup, but he soon put the cup down and began walking back and forth in the room. Kate recalled their long detention on the stools, and did not object to his perambulations. That he was able to pace was, after all, something to be grateful for, something which must never have been far from his consciousness.

"Just as Charles decided that, with revenge in his power, there was no point in, like Shylock, trying to exact it, so I have in the last days examined my life freed from whatever compulsion or obsession has, as I now see, been the guiding motive behind everything. Behind the whole of my life. Everything I told you before, though not untrue, was tinged with madness. It is as Claudius said of Hamlet: 'There's something in his soul O'er which his melancholy sits on brood.' I've been reading *Hamlet*; another obsessed soul."

Kate wanted to say that Hamlet was not an obsessed soul, but this was hardly the moment. Anyway, there would never be agreement about Hamlet; he would always speak to those in danger of acting less nobly than they knew. Jay, it was clear, was confessing, not to Kate and Reed, but as one confessed to an agent of God qualified to bestow absolution.

"What became clear to me is that my whole life, since I left your mother, was driven by anger. The object of my anger shifted onto other targets, but its source was the same. I wanted to make anyone I could reach, anyone I could envy, feel that same hopeless anger. Oh, there were calmer years, particularly during the restoration work. But even there, the pettiness, the selfishness of those affected by our work fed my outrage though they had no part in the loss of Louise—your mother," he added, as though Kate might not know of whom he spoke. Kate thought how here, as in the ice cream parlor, it was she who was being addressed, she who was the intended listener.

"I helped my friend to steal the Shakespeare picture of Prospero and Miranda out of anger. And it was anger that allowed me to join Charles in his biggest theft of all, the one in which he shot the guard. We had run into one another by chance. But have you noticed, we only say 'by chance' when the outcome of that chance seems destined, not accidental? Anyway, he urged me to come along on this job. Again, a small museum, smaller anyway than the huge ones. Again, a strike against the rich, that sort of thing. His persuasions hardly matter. It allowed me to give vent to my anger. It was an assault against the Fanslers and their narrow, tidy, safe world. Not that I would have admitted that at the time; no, my motive, if I questioned it at all, was to reclaim art for those who deserved to own it. I know this makes no sense; I've come to see that I was ready to take revenge on life by any means offered.

"This second museum theft with Charles went off just fine; the guards were stupid, easily fooled, and the pictures were not protected with individual alarms. Charles, as you might guess, was by this time highly efficient at stealing paintings. He was going to ask for ransom as usual in this case; so he told me. He offered me a small portion of the proceeds, which I refused; profiting from my anger was not to be thought of. And then another guard appeared; it was not clear where he had come from at the time—that all came out in the trial—but he had a gun and was about to call the police while keeping his gun turned on Charles. I wasn't there at that moment; I soon appeared, however, and distracted the guard for a moment. It was the chance Charles needed; he shot him. He had never injured anyone before; it all happened so quickly. I had to be sure he didn't shoot anyone else; he had to be put away for the sake of society. That's what I told myself. I need some water; does anyone else?"

Kate and Reed shook their heads, as Jay went into the kitchen. They heard him turn on the tap and drink; he refilled the glass, carried it into the living room and, putting it down, went on with his pacing and his story.

"I didn't testify against him to keep him from further crime; at least, that was hardly my main excuse. There was also the fact I learned later that he had not intended to demand ransom for the painting; he planned to sell it through the illegal art market, where enormous sums might be made. But the truth is I was furious at him for telling Fansler about, well, about you, Kate. I wanted a way to inflict injury on him, and I found it. Please don't think I wasn't appalled by the death of the guard. When you come to see that your whole life has been a case of one motive beneath all motives, that doesn't

222

mean that the more obvious incentives for one's actions are altogether false."

"Of course not," Reed said, to say something. Kate seemed lost in thought.

"That's it, really. That's what I had to say. Charles wasn't supposed to be paroled; I wasn't expected to leave Witness Protection. I never supposed that we would meet again. I also didn't grasp that he could become as obsessed with my betrayal as I had become with your mother's. Nor did I admit that your mother had reason in defense of our behavior; not my reason, but reason nonetheless. That's it, then. No, that's not quite it; there was, I learned after you left the ice cream parlor, one other hidden rage: Charles'. When his marriage was revealing itself as a disaster, and I was passionately in love, he envied me. We were old friends; he had always said I was too straight to be believed; he used to say I gave the concept of virtue a bad name. And then, when I found a love, a woman I could share all my life with while he had been entrapped by clever sham, by artificiality, his envy expanded. Those are the motives that entrapped and condemned us both."

"What now?" Reed asked, after some minutes of silence.

"For me, some attempt, somehow, at restitution. But how? Direct restitution is seldom possible, but one can turn where help is needed. Charles is both more and less fortunate. He did not shoot me, which redeems him; he told me, however, that he had hated me almost from the day of his wedding, when he saw me and your mother meet. I pointed out how

223

long ago that was. 'Yes,' he said, 'and for you, it is as powerful a moment as though it had been yesterday.' I can't make it up to you, Kate. There is nothing to make up except my ill-timed appearance so late in your life, and the dangers I unintentionally brought with me; no evil motives there. I can't make it up to the Fanslers; your brothers did me no harm; your father and mother are long dead."

"Why did you reappear then?" Kate asked.

"I liked walking in on your brother Laurence and giving him the shock of his life. My reasons were not good, but I don't think he believed me; not at first, not without irrefutable evidence, which rather lessened the shock. Why did I want to meet you? I never intended to place you in danger; you must believe that. But perhaps I guessed, or hoped, or dreamed that meeting you might bring me peace. It did, but not quite as simply as I had anticipated. Shall I get us more tea?" he asked after a pause.

Kate said that she would like a hot cup of tea. Reed gazed at her with some concern. He could not tell how rocked she had been by these revelations. It was hardly fair of Jay to use her as a confessor, but who else was there? He had already told them enough of the story so that he did not have to start at the beginning. He could speak of his revelation, his new understanding, his breakthrough one might call it, to those already at home in the context of his life.

When Jay returned with the cups of hot tea—the house did not seem equipped with a teapot, or perhaps he didn't know how to use it—they sat quietly, recovering, as though they had taken part in a particularly strenuous athletic event; a race, perhaps. There was nothing meaningful to say.

Soon Kate and Reed rose and said they must be going. Jay walked with them to the door.

"How long can you stay in this apartment?" Reed asked.

"I've a while longer. Then, who knows. Perhaps I'll just move from apartment to apartment, subletting for months at a time. I've never, at least not before or after the Witness Protection Program, been any good at putting down roots. I suppose it's significant that only when I was not myself, but living as a quite other person, that I achieved a somewhat rooted, conventional life. Enough already." He smiled.

"And how will you two be?" he asked.

"We have roots," Reed said. "We will go home and cultivate them."

"Does one cultivate roots?" Kate lightly asked; she always quibbled about word usage.

They laughed. Reed and Kate both were thinking that what they had assumed to be Kate's roots had turned out not to be quite as they supposed. But they had no intention of getting into that subject now. Saying goodbye once more, they walked down the hall toward the elevator; they heard the door of Jay's apartment close behind them.

"What I want," Kate said to Reed in the elevator, "is a swinging singles sort of bar. We'll sit on stools and pretend we've only just met and are indulging in the sort of chatter people who have just met indulge in."

"So be it," Reed said, and taking her hand, placed it under his arm as they strolled along.

*Good plays prove the better by
the help of a good epilogue.*

Epilogue

JAY DID FIND another apartment to sublet when
his lease was up; he seemed no closer than he had
ever been to wanting his own home, or his own
furniture. The places he rented were well-enough
equipped and comfortable; that casual, marginal
way of life suited him. As Reed pointed out to Kate,
he might not have had the most honest of résumés,
but he certainly had an impressive collection of references as a tenant.

For Kate and Reed, life too settled down, though
in their same apartment with the same furniture
Laurence had found so shabby. Janice had, at Laurence's insistence, called Kate and offered to help
her redecorate, but Kate refused, she hoped not un-
graciously. The ostentatious evidence of wealth had
never appealed to Kate. Perhaps she carried this too
far, or perhaps this was the only indisputable evidence of Jay's genes. And unlike the Fanslers, whose
wealth hardly needed displaying, she did not be-

lieve that there were any fashionable standards of dress and decoration that one ignored at one's peril.

As to their relation with Jay, in time that became a family sort of thing, intermittent, often spontaneous. They, or Kate alone, met with him now and then on Sunday afternoons. Sometimes they sat around and talked; often, even in winter, Kate and Jay walked with Banny in the park. When some legal question arose in Jay's life, he felt able to ask Reed for advice; the advice was gladly given.

As Kate had quoted to Reed: "Things past redress are now with me past care." By which she meant, she told him, that it all seemed now like a dream. Nor was there any need to talk of all or any part of what had happened from the day of Jay's appearance to the present moment. In New York, that city of wanderers and of friends passing, without design, in and out of intimacy, neither the unheralded appearance of an aging relative nor his exact relation to Kate seemed to require explanation.

In all the meetings between the three of them, or any two of them, they did not speak of the past, except as occasional anecdotes illuminated the exchange of the moment. Indeed, Kate was pleased to note, their conversation was light, ranging over many subjects, moving effortlessly from one topic to another.

What had gone before was, as Prospero had cautioned, the stuff of dreams.

Look for these exciting novels
of suspense by
Amanda Cross

HONEST DOUBT

A Kate Fansler Mystery

Professor Charles Haycock is dead from a
hearty dose of his own heart medication. The
mystery is not why Haycock was murdered—
very few could stomach the woman-hating
prof—but who did the deed.

Estelle Woodhaven, a private investigator
hired to find the killer, naturally enlists the
help of amateur sleuth, Kate Fansler.
Together, they start to pull at the loose ends
of the tangled Clifton College English
Department. And as the women defuse the
host of literary landmines set out for them,
Estelle suspects they're only scratching the
surface of a very large and sinister plot. . . .

Published by Fawcett
Available wherever books are sold

THE THEBAN MYSTERIES

A Kate Fansler Mystery

"If by some cruel oversight you haven't discovered Amanda Cross, you have an uncommon pleasure in store for you."

—*The New York Times Book Review*

For a century, wealthy New York girls have been trained for the rigors of upper class life at the Theban, an exclusive private school on the Upper East Side of Manhattan. Kate Fansler is lured back to her alma mater to teach a seminar on *Antigone*. But a hostile note addressed to Kate, the uniform mistrustfulness of her six, bright students, and the Dobermans that patrol the building at night suggest trouble on the spot. As Kate leads her class through the inexorable tragic unfolding of *Antigone*, a parallel nightmare envelops the school and everyone connected with it. . . .

Published by Fawcett
Available wherever books are sold

THE PUZZLED HEART

HEART

A Kate Fansler Mystery

"Intelligent . . . Literate . . . Kate is right
on the ball."
—*The New York Times Book Review*

Kate Fansler's husband, Reed, has been kidnapped—and will be killed unless Kate
obeys the directives of a ransom note.
Tormented by her own puzzled heart, Kate
seeks solace and wise counsel from both old
friends and new. But who precisely is the
enemy? The questions mount as Kate search-
es for Reed—accompanied by her trusty new
companion, a Saint Bernard puppy named
Bancroft. Hovering near Kate and Bancroft
are rampant cruelties and calculated menace.
The moment is ripe for murder.

Published by Fawcett
Available wherever books are sold

Mystery on the Internet

**Subscribe to the
MYSTERY ON THE INTERNET
e-newsletter—and receive all these
fabulous online features directly in
your e-mail inbox:**

☠ Previews of upcoming books

☠ In-depth interviews with mystery authors
and publishing insiders

☠ Calendars of signings and readings for
Ballantine mystery authors

☠ Profiles of mystery authors

☠ Mystery quizzes and contests

Two easy ways to subscribe:
Go to **www.ballantinebooks.com/mystery**
or send a blank e-mail to
join-mystery@list.randomhouse.com.

Mystery on the Internet—
the mystery e-newsletter brought to you
by Ballantine Books